RED LET[obscured]

Three sto[obscured]
by three sizz[obscured]

ALISON [obscured]
"Kent's gIRL-gEAR series triumphs with...
complex, rich characters whose scorching
chemistry will keep readers guessing!"
—*Romantic Times*

KAREN ANDERS
"Karen Anders delivers a wonderfully sexy
story with sophisticated characters whose
passion will singe your fingertips!"
—*Romantic Times*

JEANIE LONDON
"A wonderful talent that makes you want to
read her stories over and over again to relive
the wonderful sensations her words evoke."
—*Affaire de Coeur*

Dear Reader,

Sometimes a glimmer of an idea turns into something wonderfully fantastic. That's what happened with *Red Letter Nights*. This collaboration was all about New Orleans, a place near and dear to all of our hearts and the perfect place to set our novellas. But there were more stories to be told, so we all have follow-up books set in Court du Chaud, the "hot" court.

But for now, here is our collaboration of eighteen months of e-mails and lengthy phone calls, ideas and magic. Magic because Christmas is a red-letter season for secret admirers, sexy gifts and love notes. A red-hot time that inspires couples to turn their fantasies into reality. And all our couples *really* want more than just one hot holiday.

Café Eros is the hub of the hot court. Tucked away from the world behind a wrought-iron gate, this gardened courtyard is *the* place to live in New Orleans' French Quarter. This anthology collection contains three blazing novellas that prove Christmas is only the start of some very red-letter nights…nights when desire is too hot to keep secret.

Enjoy,

Alison Kent

Karen Anders

Jeanie London

RED LETTER NIGHTS

BY
ALISON KENT
KAREN ANDERS
JEANIE LONDON

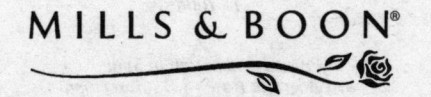

MILLS & BOON

DID YOU PURCHASE THIS BOOK WITHOUT A COVER?
If you did, you should be aware it is **stolen property** as it was reported *unsold and destroyed* by a retailer. Neither the author nor the publisher has received any payment for this book.

All the characters in this book have no existence outside the imagination of the author, and have no relation whatsoever to anyone bearing the same name or names. They are not even distantly inspired by any individual known or unknown to the author, and all the incidents are pure invention.

All Rights Reserved including the right of reproduction in whole or in part in any form. This edition is published by arrangement with Harlequin Enterprises II B.V. The text of this publication or any part thereof may not be reproduced or transmitted in any form or by any means, electronic or mechanical, including photocopying, recording, storage in an information retrieval system, or otherwise, without the written permission of the publisher.

This book is sold subject to the condition that it shall not, by way of trade or otherwise, be lent, resold, hired out or otherwise circulated without the prior consent of the publisher in any form of binding or cover other than that in which it is published and without a similar condition including this condition being imposed on the subsequent purchaser.

MILLS & BOON and MILLS & BOON with the Rose Device are registered trademarks of the publisher.

First published in Great Britain 2006 by Harlequin Mills & Boon Limited, Eton House, 18-24 Paradise Road, Richmond, Surrey TW9 1SR

RED LETTER NIGHTS © 2005 by Harlequin Books S.A.

The publisher acknowledges the copyright holders of the individual works as follows:

*Luv U Madly © Mica Stone 2005
Deliver Me © Karen Alarie 2005
Signed, Sealed, Seeduced © Jeanie LeGendre 2005*

*ISBN-13: 978 0 263 84616 4
ISBN-10: 0 263 84616 4*

14-1006

*Printed and bound in Spain
by Litografia Rosés S.A., Barcelona*

To Karen & Jeanie for inviting me along on the
trip to New Orleans! But especially to Walt.
It may take a while, but I never fail to
use what you give me.
—Alison Kent

To Jeanie London for her support,
laughter and great friendship. To Alison Kent for her
wonderful twisted way of looking at things, which
makes me chuckle just when I need to. Thanks for
coming along for this fantastic ride!
—Karen Anders

To my Court du Chaud collaborators—
Karen Anders and Alison Kent. Working with
you both has been a thrill and a pleasure. ;-)
—Jeanie London

CONTENTS

LUV U MADLY 9
Alison Kent

DELIVER ME 97
Karen Anders

SIGNED, SEALED, SEDUCED 173
Jeanie London

LUV U MADLY

BY
ALISON KENT

1

CLAIRE BRADEN couldn't remember a hotter day coming this close to Christmas in any of the places she'd lived during her thirty-one years. Whatever had possessed her to move to New Orleans was an inspiration that had long since melted into a puddle of sticky goo.

The temperature was unbearable, though it wasn't the heat as much as the stifling humidity. The sort of sweltering, wet-blanket air that had her dreaming of walking naked through her town house and eating fresh fruit over the kitchen sink.

Running her air conditioner in December seemed such a sin, but run it she would—if only it wasn't in need of repair. And she hated the thought of parting with that much cash until the heat took up seasonal residence late in May.

A cold front would blow through soon. She believed that with all of her heart. Besides, it was the holiday season. Surely Santa had received her wish list already.

The air conditioner. The Kooba slouchy shoulder bag in plum, please. Ten more hours in every day. Ten less pounds around her hips. Oh, and a fling with the guy whose balcony at Number 13 in the Court du Chaud sat kitty-corner to hers.

The first was practical, necessary, hardly a treat; the second a reward with which she'd be spoiling herself once she billed her current image-consulting client. The third, a pipe dream, the fourth her inherited lot in life.

The fifth, on the other hand, was extravagant, unexpected, a gift she wanted way more than she needed. It was also a gift that would go a long way toward assuaging the full-blown case of lust she had in her heart.

Unlocking her courtyard-facing front door, she let herself into the town house's entry foyer. The outside heat and humidity were nothing in the scheme of things. Her new neighbor was the number one source of her blood running hot.

She'd been living at Court du Chaud for two years, yet knew very few of the other residents. Establishing her business as a corporate image consultant would have been even longer in coming had she not arrived in New Orleans with a portfolio of high-profile businesses whose executive offices she'd made over, as well as client consultations already scheduled as the result of referrals from past jobs done well.

As it was, the hours she poured into work came from the same pitcher as the hours left for sleep and socializing. She hadn't yet mastered that never-ending loaves-and-fishes magic. And as much as she enjoyed dating and making new friends, sleep was what kept her running at this pace.

She *had* gotten to know Perry Brazille who lived across the court. The two women often ate breakfast together at Café Eros, the two-story eatery at the courtyard's entrance, drinking coffee, splitting one of the rich pastries that neither of them needed, comparing notes on their romantic dry spells.

And while at the café, Claire had picked up enough tidbits of gossip—most of those from the court busybody, Madame Alain—and enough snippets of conversation to know her new male neighbor would fill her straight-sex, no-emotional-involvement-fling bill nicely.

He'd paid cash for his town house, drove an import that cost a four-year tuition, dressed in suits that had never seen a rack, and had that rock-star smolder that caused women to throw panties and scream.

And, yes. It was terribly out of character for her to be drawn by external trappings when her business was all about image and she knew better than most what a fresh coat of paint could hide.

In fact, she gave herself a refurbishing makeover at every opportunity, trying on different looks as if she'd be able to find the source of her personal discontent once she hit on the right combination of color and style.

But her neighbor was hot and sexy and built like a god, and there were times nothing else mattered. Times like now with the holidays approaching when she wasn't so crazy about spending the days alone.

After kicking off her Prada pumps, she peeled off her panty hose, then tossed them, her purse and her navy blazer onto her overstuffed sofa colored in oriental reds and golds, and headed into the kitchen for a tall glass of iced tea.

Her sleeveless white blouse unbuttoned over her ivory silk camisole, she retrieved her leather attaché and the day's mail she'd tucked down inside, and made her way upstairs to her bedroom's balcony.

The cane fan overhead stirred the sluggish air; she sat in one chair at the glass-and-black wrought-iron table, propped her feet on a second, dropped her attaché onto the third. It didn't take her long to sort through the mail.

Flyers, catalogues, postcards and sales sheets went into one stack for the trash. Bills went into her Day-Timer, as did her tickets to see the Black Eyed Peas in March. That left half a dozen Christmas cards that she settled in to read with her cold drink.

Three were from Windy, Tess and Alexandra, the women who made up her core circle of confidantes. They'd attended and graduated University of Texas together, still vacationed together and tried each year to coordinate their holiday greetings.

This year, unfortunately, Claire was suffering from overcoordination. She hadn't even found time to buy cards, forget personalizing, addressing and mailing them.

A shame, too, because reading the handwritten notes from her girlfriends, even though she talked to them at least once a week and exchanged e-mails with each more often, brought a silly smile to her face.

Seeing their handwriting, imagining where they'd been sitting when they'd dashed off the words, picturing their quirky habits—Windy tugging on the ends of her hair, Tess requiring a certain fountain pen, Alex keeping one eye on the task, her attention on her computer screen and a role-playing game…

Claire sighed. First thing tomorrow she was stopping for cards. For her girlfriends, her family. Enough even for the neighbors she *had* gotten to know. Chloe who owned the café. Josie, the social worker living in number sixteen. Perry who seemed to run on Claire's same manic schedule.

Hmm. Maybe she'd even slip one underneath the door

belonging to the object of her lustful affection. Welcome him to the neighborhood properly and all that. Invite him over for a holiday drink. Keep the introductions sweet and simple and…sweaty.

At the sound of his balcony door opening, Claire forced her attention to her drink and the rest of her mail. She didn't think he'd ever caught her out here looking her best. And lately, with the heat…she grimaced. Imagining what he'd see should he glance over hardly got her hopes up.

But then she thought twice. She'd had a great pedicure over the weekend, and was waxed, trimmed and plucked smooth way beyond where the hem of her skirt had settled high on her upper thighs.

Her blond chignon was no longer as sleek as it had been this morning. The humidity had taken its toll; stray wisps blew around her face thanks to the overhead fan, adding to her look of coming undone.

Her camisole was lacy, her skin sticking to the silk, the cups of her bra pushing up and shaping as advertised. The overall look was one more *Maxim* model than corporate image consultant, but it was also one suited to her mission of indulging in a holiday fling.

Overt sexuality was not her personal style. At least not when it came to an outward display. She enjoyed subtlety; a hint of skin went a lot further in her book than nudity. She preferred a quick flick of a tongue wetting lips to a mouth sucking on a lollipop.

The glimpse of a man's chest in the open neck of his shirt. An expensive watch on a hair-dusted wrist. Both of those got to her in ways biker shorts or rippling abs did not. And a gaze cut short by a flutter of lashes hit her a whole lot harder than a long hungry stare.

Yet even as those thoughts crossed her mind, she felt her neighbor visually taking her measure. She pulled her feet from the chair and reached for her attaché. As she did, her blouse gaped open but only for a second, maybe a fraction more.

Then she stood, leaning forward to tuck her Day-Timer and the cards she hadn't finished reading down inside the leather case, knowingly exposing her cleavage above her camisole.

That done, she picked up her glass of iced tea and moved to stand at the balcony's railing, looking down at the twinkle of colored lights on the Christmas tree in the courtyard below, and letting her thoughts run wild.

She imagined her neighbor standing behind her, felt the heat of his body that was so much larger than her own, absorbed his strength as she leaned back against him.

She fantasized about the touch of his hands, his broad palms skimming up her bare arms, her skin pebbling, her hair standing on end.

The reality of her body's reaction should not have been the surprise that it was. Her breasts tightened. Her sex tingled. She drank some of her tea, finding it difficult to swallow, much less move.

The condensation from the glass dripped onto her throat; the dampness did little to cool her because, as she turned to go in… She made a huge mistake and glanced over to the next balcony.

His balcony.

He stood in the doorway, hands shoved in the pockets of the day's dark suit pants, his tie loosened at his neck, the sleeves of his white dress shirt cuffed to midarm.

His chest rose and fell heavily, his pulse popped at the

base of his throat. With his jaw set tight, his temple throbbing, he looked the picture of a man barely restrained.

She forgot how to breathe. In that instant, she felt as if she would never again need food or water or air. Only him. She would need only him. And as self-sufficient as she was, as independent—living on her own, pursuing her goals with only the occasional encouraging "attagirl" from her circle of friends—the thought of needing a man for anything left her reeling.

Especially a man she didn't even know.

RANDY HAD NEVER intended to stay at the office so long. Yes, he'd been working late every night for several weeks. But he'd determined tonight would be the night of change. The night to take back his life.

The night to get home, pour a drink and head out onto the balcony to wait. To see if she'd show as she had yesterday, if they'd make that same connection. The one that had nearly forced him to his knees.

She didn't make an appearance every night, but lately, the heat and the Christmas tree in the courtyard below drove her outside more often.

The fan hanging over her balcony stirred the heavy air. He knew that because his fan did the same.

The lights on the tree he only noticed because of the way she watched them, the way they sparkled like colored gems in her white-blond hair, the way they brought a smile to her mouth—one he didn't think he'd ever seen reach her eyes.

It didn't seem to be sadness that kept it away, but focus. As if she didn't have time in her schedule for distractions of any sort. And that intrigued him because it reminded him so much of himself.

He'd heard gossip about her air conditioner being on the fritz. It sucked for her sake, but he definitely liked the way she looked all hot and messed up. She was the type of woman who made him think about sex that went a lot farther than sharing a nice dinner and then getting off.

Looking the way she'd looked last night had him weighing the pros and cons of having her at her place or his. His with cool sheets and pebbled gooseflesh. Hers with nothing but hot skin on skin. The answer required no obvious thought. All he needed was a way in.

His own town house had been gutted by the previous owner and now consisted of a downstairs great room and an upstairs loft. He made his way to the kitchen area's island counter, dropping off the mail he'd picked up from the floor by the front door's drop slot before grabbing a cold beer from the fridge.

He then reached for the room's main remote control panel, hit the button for the corner lamp and the one for the big-screen TV, flipping to ESPN before glancing at the stack of mail.

Longneck bottle halfway to his mouth, he stopped, his attention snagged by a red envelope, no stamp, no address. The size of a small card or invitation. He picked it up, turned it over. The flap was unglued.

Curiosity got the better of him. He set his beer on the black marble countertop, pulled the card from the sleeve and read.

It may look a lot like Christmas, but it feels like the Fourth of July. I have fans. I have ice. Wanna share? I'll leave the door open. Say 10:00 p.m.? And, by the way, I prefer no strings. And no questions.

Blood running hot beneath the surface of his skin, he read it for a second time, then a third, then had the presence of mind to glance at his watch.

Eight-thirty. He had time to shower, shave, change clothes and decide on a bottle of wine. No strings and no questions. Wondering what her reasons were for the conditions, he decided he'd give her that for now.

But only for now.

CLAIRE STOOD on her balcony watching the lights twinkle on the Christmas tree in the courtyard below.

The last time she'd looked at the clock in her bedroom, it had been nine-thirty-five.

She'd thought about slowly counting to sixty over and over for twenty-five minutes, but changed her mind when she tripped herself up first time out.

Will he or won't he?

He wants me; he wants me not.

She'd written the card while still parked in the lot of the gift shop, having shopped on her way home from work. The plan was to slip the invitation into his mail slot before she second-guessed herself.

What she should have done was write out the cards for her girlfriends first and imagine their responses to her scheme that was so wildly out of character. Claire the safe one, the practical one, the boring, predictable one.

Instead, she'd let herself be swayed by a gorgeous man in gorgeous trappings, knowing full well she was buying into the myth of beauty being more than skin deep. Sure, it could happen. But really, what were the odds?

In her experience, very slim. The men she'd known who were yummy enough to eat knew it—and weren't the least bit shy about strutting their studly stuff. Totally unattractive. Horribly gauche. Hardly traits about which to write home.

Traits that reminded her exactly why she needed to close her eyes and open her mind, to find a man who made her think and laugh and wonder how she'd lived without him in her life.

And she was still pondering all that strutting and how it always ended up going nowhere and was so unappealing and made the whole dating process such a huge waste of time, when she heard the opening and closing of her front door.

She froze, her heart pumping so fast and so furiously that her chest ached with the strain.

Her lashes drifted down; with her eyes shut, she found herself listening for the tiniest sounds, and still she swore she felt more than heard the echo of his footsteps on the stairs.

She'd changed from the day's navy business suit into a lightweight yellow tank dress earlier in the evening, after a cool citrus-scented bath and an even colder shower.

But now the fabric itched her skin, hugged her too tightly, clung in all the wrong places, made her sweat.

Or so she tried to make herself believe when she knew the truth was anticipation. And the rest of the truth was that even with her eyes closed, she was still seeing twinkling lights that had nothing to do with Christmas.

It was when he stepped onto the balcony that she looked out over the courtyard again. She didn't turn, simply listened to the clink of two glasses on the table, the heavier thunk of a bottle of wine.

Even when he walked up behind her, when her skin

pebbled from his nearness and from nerves, she continued to face forward, her fingers curled over the balcony's railing, an anchor in a storm.

She felt an intense need to hold on, felt as if she was being swept away, was falling, slipping, losing herself in the anonymity of what she'd created, what she'd thought she wanted, what she was certain she still did.

He moved in, closer. She felt his body's heat, the vibration of tension tightening the air. When he passed beneath the ceiling fan, his shadow fell over her body. And the facade of personal space disappeared.

Breathing was no longer a luxury but a struggle she tried to hide. He settled his hands on her shoulders, squeezed, leaned in close to her ear and whispered, "Is this what you want?"

Was having him here the purpose of her invitation? Yes. Was the way he was making her tremble what she'd expected? No. Was the whole of it, the *this* he was asking about, what she wanted?

She nodded, answered, "Yes."

He slid his hands down her bare arms to her elbows, her wrists, holding her hands, massaging the center of her palms with his thumbs.

"I understand the 'no strings.' But why the 'no questions'?"

"Because I don't want to talk." She wanted to know him as a lover, not as a friend, and was doing what men had done for eons, objectifying a member of the opposite sex for nothing more than pleasure.

But she was also taking into consideration the nature of the female beast to judge physical encounters on an emotional scale, as well as her busy life that left no time for involvement running that deep.

She shrugged, her shoulders scraping over the fabric of his shirt. He was so big behind her, yet not for a second did she feel a threat.

Instead she felt strangely safe. "I just don't want to talk."

He leaned forward, his breath teasing the hair over her ear as he asked, "Then why are you?"

Good question. One with a very simple answer. An answer that fell into the category of being careful about what one wished for.

Diving into the deep end of the pool, she held her breath and said, "Because I don't know where to start."

2

HER WHISPERED ANSWER raised all manner of red flags.

What sort of woman was Claire Braden—Randy had learned her name when he'd learned of her air conditioner troubles—that she could be so bold with her invitation yet such a bundle of nerves when he arrived to accept?

He laced their fingers together, wrapped their stacked arms around her waist, pulled her back into his body and breathed in the soft scent of her perfume.

She smelled warm and lush and fertile and alive—a combination that had him breathing deeply again, had him holding back a shudder.

"We can start with a glass of wine," he finally suggested, sensing her need to relax, recognizing—and fighting not to lose—his own dwindling control.

"That would be nice," she said, shivering as he rubbed his thumbs over the lower swells of her breasts.

When she groaned, he changed his mind. "Or we can start with a kiss."

She laughed at that, a light airy chuckle that had him aching to hear more. "That would be nice, too."

He started to spin her around, wanting to learn her mouth, the texture of her lips, to feel her tongue slide over his, but he waited because he knew keeping this encounter as impersonal as she wanted wasn't possible.

She needed to understand the truth that this would never be casual sex. Not with the heat spiraling between them. Not with the way she responded to his touch.

Not with his appetite for acquiring expensive and beautiful things.

He wanted her. He would want her for more than one night. Getting her to understand that was paramount. "What I think we really need to start with is a new set of rules."

She stiffened a bit where he held her. "Oh, really?"

He nodded, his cheek rubbing against her soft hair. "You know as well as I do that we have to talk."

"I suppose," she hedged, leaning her head back into the crook of his shoulder and sighing heavily. "Though I was really hoping to do no more than feel."

A woman with a sensuous nature to go with her stunning good looks. She'd invited him up to her place for fun and games, and he was insisting they talk. Hell if he didn't deserve to have his man-card revoked.

He released her hands, ran his palms down her rib cage to her hips, worked his thumbs up along her spine, massaged his way to her neck. Her curves were amazing, lush and toned and the perfect fit for his hands.

And though his body tightened, he held himself in check. They had time. They had all night. As far as he was concerned, they had months into the future to enjoy what they'd started.

What they didn't have was a single reason to rush.

She moaned, her head fell forward, and she said, "Yeah, feeling. Like that."

Smiling silently, he moved in, trapping her between the balcony railing and his body, pressing her dangerously close to the edge.

He wanted her own senses to run as hot as his. He wanted her to sizzle with the same lethal thrill beginning to eat him alive.

This wasn't going to be a quick and easy lay. He'd known that last night when their gazes had locked for those few seconds that had gone on forever.

And because of that, because—he reminded himself—they had time, he let her go and backed away, heading to the table to pour them both a drink.

When he looked up, he found that she'd turned and now stood with her back to the courtyard. He couldn't see her eyes; the light on the fan didn't reach that far, the one from the bedroom was dimmed by the sheer drapes covering the balcony doors.

He stayed where he was, reached out to offer her a glass of wine. To take it, she'd have to step forward. To move closer, to come to him.

She did, but slowly, pushing away from the railing, gliding the balcony's width.

Her simple dress, the pastel yellow a perfect complement to her near white hair, draped her body as if it were designer wear instead of the same cotton fabric as the black T-shirt he wore. The lines caressed her breasts and hips; his palms tingled, the base of his spine burned.

She took the wineglass from his hand, brought it to her lips and sipped, doing so without ever releasing his gaze.

Moments ago she'd seemed uncertain. Now what he saw in her eyes was anything but hesitation or second thoughts. What it was was a challenge.

And he would never have made it as far as he had in life by failing to accept.

He brought his own glass to his mouth, maintaining eye contact as he swallowed. And then, ignoring the basic rules she'd set, asked her the one question he was most curious to have her answer.

"Why me?"

"Do you want me to be honest?" she responded even though he wasn't sticking to the deal upon which she'd insisted. Then again, neither was she. "Or do you want me to be nice?"

He stared at her for one long moment, then laughed.

She saw it begin in his eyes; tiny laugh lines appeared, barely visible in the glow from the fan's light above him. She saw it next in the dimples that bracketed his lips.

But it was the sound he let go, a great gust of amusement, a severing of the tension around which they'd been dancing, that grabbed hold of her heart and squeezed.

Yes. Her heart. The very organ she'd determined to keep out of his bed.

From an emotional standpoint, this encounter was not going the way she'd wanted. His fault for the laugh. Her fault for being susceptible.

Physically, however, she held out great hope that the sparks between them had only just begun to fly. "I'll take that to mean honesty works for you?"

"I wouldn't have it any other way," he said and raised his glass in a toast.

She settled into the closest chair, pretending to relax as she crossed her legs, letting her dangling foot swing. "I like the way you look."

"Well, that's certainly honest," he replied, taking the chair opposite hers, leaning back, stretching out his legs and crossing his ankles.

"Too much so?" she asked, running her index finger around the rim of her glass and adding, "Would you prefer I be subtle? That I approach you in a bar? Or offer to buy you a cup of coffee at Café Eros? We could flirt and make small talk. You could wonder about my intent. I could pretend to think about letting you take me home."

He'd set his wineglass on the table while she talked, and now held it in place with two fingers threaded around the stem, his palm flat on the base.

She studied the dark hair dusting his wrist and the far edge of his hand. Then she wondered how close the crystal was to breaking; he was so very rigid, his body so very hard and still.

"That all seems like such a waste of time," he finally said, to which she replied, "I agree."

And then she waited, her heart beating hard, and watched him nod, watched him pick up his wineglass and drink, watched him watch her all the while.

It was a strange sort of cat and mouse they were playing, a game that if done right meant two winners, a game that if done perfectly would mean no regrets, no heartache.

No heartbreak.

She'd served the ball into his court. The next move was his, and he made it by asking her, "So, Claire, where do we go from here?"

Of course he would know her name, she mused. He didn't look to be the sort of man who overlooked details—especially those that gave him the upper hand.

"Since I haven't had the pleasure…"

"Randy," he said, inclining his head.

She'd expected something more highbrow, a name with a Roman numeral at the end. Randy was so all-American approachable, so boy-next-door. Exactly what he was, she thought with a smile—a smile that he mirrored, and the tension returned.

"You haven't answered my question," he reminded her.

"I'm pretty sure the ground rules made clear that I wouldn't be answering anything."

He returned his glass to the table, slowly lifted his gaze to meet hers. "The first was just an exception then? Exercising your female prerogative?"

She stared down into her wine colored like winter sunshine. "That would imply that I'd changed my mind."

"And you haven't."

She shook her head.

"About anything."

This time, before she did, she looked up and made him wait until the pulse at his temple pounded.

"Good," he said and held out a hand. "Then come over here and kiss me."

Awareness of the space between them, the very short distance she'd have to cross to do as he wanted—as she wanted—stirred in her belly, more potent than the alcohol already settling there.

She uncrossed her legs, set her glass on the balcony's surface, letting the neck of her dress gape to reveal the sheer cups of her bra. Then she got to her feet and reached out, touching her fingertips to his.

He refused the simple contact, enclosing her wrist in the circle of his fingers and thumb, pulling her forward to stand between his spread legs before pulling her down.

She settled her weight lightly on his thigh, but he wasn't having any of that either. No. He tugged her into his body, forced her into the crook of his elbow.

She had no choice. She wrapped her arms around his neck and held on.

He didn't lower his mouth as she'd expected. Instead, he used his free hand to caress her cheekbones, her jaw, the length of her throat to the hollow where she felt the telltale beat of her heart, the curves of her breasts beneath the tank's ribbed cotton.

Her breath caught and her nipples hardened. And beneath her thighs she felt his reaction that was unmistakably thick and hard.

"Did you know that you have great eyes?"

"Bausch and Lomb," she said in response.

He shook his head. "Not the color. The clarity. The sparkle. Your eyes are…rich."

"Rich. Hmm. I think that's the best come-on I've ever heard."

Even so, she couldn't help but think back to last night, to the way they'd connected, to the need for him she'd felt that left her unable to sleep, that made her past experiences with men seem like time spent in a child's sandbox.

He touched the pad of his thumb to her lower lip in a way that was all grown-up. "I thought we'd skipped the come-on step."

He was right. They had. They'd skipped a lot of other steps between here and there, too. Steps she'd always thought so necessary, yet so incredibly dull.

"We did," she said, threading her fingers into the hair that just brushed his nape, feeling a shudder in the hand that still caressed her. "I'm just not good with compliments."

"With accepting them? Or believing them?"

Sigh. What was she doing, telling him personal details, letting him worm his way beneath the surface of this encounter?

She'd wanted anonymity. Two bodies doing that thing that two bodies do, nothing more than the pleasure of that. And so she finally answered him in the only way she could.

She pulled his mouth to hers.

His chuckle tickled her but only for a moment because his laughter quickly dissolved into a groan that rolled up from his gut. She felt it in his thighs where she sat in his lap. She felt it in his arms that held her.

But more than in his limbs, she felt it in his lips pressed to hers, his tongue seeking entrance. He tasted like the wine they'd drank, like the metallic charge of electricity, like she wanted him.

He caught at her lips, nibbled, sucked, slid his tongue over hers to play. She held his head and played, too, stroking her fingers over his ear, her tongue over his teeth. The fan overhead did nothing to quell the temperature rising between them like a helium balloon.

He shifted beneath her, adjusting his erection, slipping his hand between their bodies to cover her breast. Her whimper filled his mouth, and he kissed her harder, rolled her nipple with his finger and thumb.

Her body was on fire. Her skin burned. Her breath scorched a path up her throat. Flames licked and toyed between her legs. And this was only a kiss. Getting naked with this man was going to kill her.

She started to pull away to tell him just that, to ask him how he felt about calling things off—or at least taking it inside to prevent the fan from scattering her ashes—but he beat her to the punch.

He left his hand where it was and lifted his head, staring down into her eyes he thought so rich. His were green, almost pine, darker than jade, his lashes the color of deep fertile soil.

And then he smiled. "I could use another drink."

"So could I." She started to push up, but he held her.

"And I'm serious about that new set of rules."

By now, she was curious enough to throw her convictions to the wind and ask. "What did you have in mind?"

"Before I leave tonight, I'll ask you one question." His eyes sparkled with mischief. "When I see you tomorrow night, you'll answer."

Tomorrow night. Interesting that he was already thinking ahead. Even more interesting that she was falling for that look in his eyes and giving in. "Quid pro quo?"

He offered a nod of concession. "If you'd like."

"I think it's only fair."

At that, the corner of his mouth quirked upward. "You believe all is fair in love and war?"

"Especially in war." She straightened in his lap, got to her feet, waited until he'd done the same then offered her hand. "Deal?"

He took it, shook it. "Deal."

Now all she could do was hope she didn't regret what she was about to do. "Then what do you want to know?"

RANDY COULDN'T BELIEVE he'd walked away without bedding her.

He'd had every intention of laying claim to the prize

she'd put on the table, of leaving her place and returning home pleased and spent.

What happened instead was he found she came with complications he needed time to process.

The fact that she was open about wanting him in her bed—this, the same woman he'd fantasized about when finding her on her balcony in total dishabille—made her that much more a compelling challenge.

He was not in the market for a relationship. That didn't mean he was blind to the benefits offered by an exclusive and intimate arrangement.

Quite frankly, he thought, staring into the open door of his fridge, having a woman like Claire around would make a lot of his life run more smoothly.

He wouldn't have to scramble to find dates for the work functions that took up so much of his time. Sure, he could attend the foundation's fund-raisers alone and often did.

But a gorgeous woman on his arm was a near guarantee that he'd be able to spend more time focused on the purpose of the evening and less fending off unwanted advances.

If that sounded arrogant, so be it, he mused, closing the refrigerator door since what he needed to satisfy his appetite wasn't inside but next door. And if he wanted any relief from what she'd left him feeling, he'd have to provide it himself.

He jogged up the stairs to his loft, jerking his T-shirt overhead on the way, toeing off his Italian leather loafers and shucking off his khakis once inside the upstairs bathroom. It was late. He needed to be asleep. Tomorrow would be another long day crunching numbers.

Peeling down his boxers, he climbed into the shower stall, turned on the water and reached for the soap. For some strange reason, however, instead of his mind drifting to work or to Claire, he found himself thinking back to his high school years in Austin, Texas.

He'd played trumpet in an ensemble with his four best friends, and not a one of them had a clue where he'd come from. The only girl in the group, Heidi Malone, had also been the only one living in a situation that would have needed a hand up to be called lower class.

His situation, before the Schneiders' intervention, would have required a shovel.

Even now, standing beneath the steaming spray in his shower stall with antique brass fixtures and marble walls colored like café au lait, he had trouble believing that he'd once lived on the streets.

That he'd shoplifted to clothe himself.

That he'd rummaged in restaurant Dumpsters to eat.

He'd been a scrapper; he'd have died of exposure otherwise, and was surprised he hadn't died by a gunshot or a knife blade or a big meaty fist.

He pushed aside the past and returned to the present, to the shower steaming the stress from his muscles and bones. Now he made sure he never lacked for anything. Clothes, food, the roof over his head, the wheels parked in his garage.

He didn't need the money his uncle Luther paid him to manage the finances for the foundation that administered educational grants and scholarship funds.

He took it because life had taught him to do so.

Taught him to indulge when he wanted because he could afford it.

Taught him to remember the days when even sleep had

been too expensive because what he'd gathered during the day could be stolen from him just as quickly.

Again, he shook off the memories, shook the water from his hair and his eyes, sputtering as he did. And then he thought back to the evening he'd just spent next door, and to having Claire in his lap.

He pictured her eyes; when he'd said they were rich, he'd been honest. He couldn't think of another word to describe the depth of what he'd seen.

Intelligence, awareness. She'd known full well what he'd expected when responding to the card she'd slipped through his door.

The fact that he'd come home after little more than kissing her, after touching her just enough to want to feel her skin without the barrier of ribbed cotton, had surprised both of them—as had her agreement to answer his question, his agreement to answer hers.

He'd asked her if the first man she'd had sex with had broken her heart. The flash of pain in her eyes had been the only answer he'd needed.

But now he couldn't wait to hear if she'd cover up what he'd seen with an abundance of words, or if her response would be as honest as what her eyes had told him.

What she ended up saying when he saw her tomorrow would play a big part in where he took this seduction, how he would work to win her over, persuade her that he could give her more than a good time in bed.

It was her question to him, however, that was giving him hell, making it impossible to get it up and find the release he needed. Stroking himself wasn't doing a thing.

Because what Claire wanted to know was what his pricey sports car and designer suits were hiding.

And how the hell could he tell her that when doing so would be admitting a truth he'd spent years pretending didn't exist?

3

IF NOT FOR FEAR of suffering heatstroke, Claire would've spent the next day working at home.

She had a small office on the second floor of a revitalized Jackson Square warehouse where she saw clients—at least the clients who didn't prefer she come to them.

Eventually, she always did.

But there was something about holding the first meeting with a prospective account on her own turf that gave her a different perspective than seeing them in their element—much as having Randy come to her place took away the crutch of the familiar for him.

Not that he'd needed any crutch at all, she mused. He'd had no trouble finding his way to her balcony, making himself at home, flipping her rules of engagement into ones that suited him better. Tonight, she'd be on her toes. She had to be or else he'd be taking over her holiday fling.

For now, she had to get back to work. She had her initial consultation with the Flatbacker Foundation scheduled for Thursday at their offices, so was spending the morning researching the firm on the Internet.

The three founding partners were in their seventies and had set up the organization over fifty years before.

The list of recipients who'd benefited from their generosity with grants and scholarships was impressive.

Finding the conservative institution located in one of downtown New Orleans' newest buildings surprised her. She'd expected a location as rich with history as the firm, and was admittedly curious about their choice of location.

The only thing she'd been told by the executive assistant booking the appointment was the new CFO felt the firm's image didn't reflect their mission statement. She was in the middle of reading that very thing when her phone rang.

She didn't even look away from her screen at the caller display. She simply answered. "First Impressions."

"I checked my mail yesterday, and nothing from you. I had a card from Windy and one from Alex. What happened?"

Claire laughed at the righteous indignation in Tess Autrey's voice. "I'm a bad, bad friend?"

"I'll say. Next time you decide to jump ship for another state, remind me to impress upon you the emotional damage you'll be inflicting upon those you leave behind."

Tess. Ever the psychologist. "It's a freakin' Christmas card, Autrey. Get over it."

"Ooh, and the snark goes on. Sounds like someone got up on the wrong side of bed."

Claire had gotten up alone, that was the problem. "I'm a grouch. It's like umpty billion degrees here, and my air conditioner isn't working. You'll have to find your Christmas spirit elsewhere."

"I think that would make you a grinch, not a grouch."

"Believe it or not, I've got cards going out in today's mail." She'd written the notes to her friends last night after

Randy had left her hot and bothered and unable to sleep. "They're right here on my desk, see?"

"No phone-o-vision on this end, sorry. Hang a sec." In the background, Tess verified an appointment with her assistant before coming back on the line. "Just checking in between patients. Anything new going on with you?"

Claire's thoughts were still on her sexy neighbor. "You mean anything new since two days ago when we talked?"

"Yeah, well, it's the holidays, and you're not here to rescue me from being at my mother's beck and call."

Dr. Georgina Autrey was a world-renowned feminist à la Gloria Steinem, and mother and daughter had never seen eye to eye on anything. Meaning Tess never got a traditional Christmas except when she spent the holiday with Claire.

Except this year Claire hadn't decorated or baked or even managed to send out her cards.

Well, cards to anyone but Randy.

"Be glad I'm not there. At least with the distance between us, you can't see what a lousy elf I've been this year."

"Yes. I can. All I have to do is check my mailbox."

"It's coming." She pointed at the stack of mail on her desk. "I swear, it's coming."

"So what's his name?"

Claire almost choked. "Whose name? Tess, we just talked two days ago."

"The day we were all buying and mailing our cards. You didn't. It must be a man."

"It wasn't. It was work."

"But there is a man."

"Sort of."

"What does that mean?"

"It's just my neighbor."

"From the balcony next door? The Michelangelo's David Adonis guy?"

He was that gorgeous, yes, but he was also so very human. She leaned back in her chair. "His name's Randy. He asked me if the first guy I slept with broke my heart."

Tess sucked in a breath. "Ouch. What did you tell him?"

"Nothing yet. I'm supposed to answer his question tonight."

"Sounds hot and kinky." Tess didn't even try to hide her sarcasm. "Not to mention horribly romantic."

Claire laughed. It was none of the above, but explaining the deal she and Randy had made, the terms of their involvement, would take more time than Tess had.

As if they were on the same wavelength, Tess came back with, "I've got to go, sweetie. Just wanted to make sure you weren't pouring eggnog into your Wheaties to get through the season."

Oh, fine. Now Claire was getting all weepy and damp. "You're a good friend, Autrey. No matter how many bad things I say about you."

"I know," Tess said and rang off, leaving Claire to daydream wistfully about the girlfriends she'd left in Houston when she'd made her upwardly mobile move—though with the imbalance between her out-box and in, she wondered if the move had truly been anything but eastwardly.

She spent the rest of the day finishing as many small tasks as she could, clearing space on her plate for the functional space analysis she'd be working on as part of the Flatbacker project should they sign on.

By the time she'd finished returning phone queries, updating her financial spreadsheets, filing and responding to business e-mails, it was almost seven.

She hadn't even taken a break for lunch, making do with a package of peanut butter crackers from the bottom of her purse and a pear from a gift basket sent by a former client.

It was time to go home, to eat something that didn't require using her oven and further heating up her house, to catch up on the hours of sleep she'd lost last night.

Ugh, but she was way too young to be this tired.

Which was why when she walked through her front door twenty minutes later, her hair drooping from the humidity, thoughts of Randy impossible to shake, she was sure she was dreaming.

The town house was cool. And it smelled wonderful, as if she'd walked into Ristorante Carmelo for dinner.

Since there was only one logical explanation, she didn't bother wondering or worrying or giving in to the initial rush of adrenaline-fueled fright.

All she did was kick off her shoes, toss her purse, her attaché, her panty hose and her suit jacket to the sofa, and follow her nose.

The smell of butter, garlic and parmesan cheese had her drooling. But the true sensory meltdown came the minute she turned the corner into the kitchen and got a good look at her cook. Wow.

Just wow.

Drooling fool that she was, those were the only words that came to mind. Randy stood in front of the sink, draining bow-tie pasta into a colander, steam rising like a devil's halo around his face.

He wore suit pants, navy, and a white dress shirt with the sleeves cuffed over his forearms. His tie hung askew over his unbuttoned collar.

Once the steam cleared, he saw her and smiled. "Is alfredo okay? Neither one of us had ingredients for marinara."

"You look like you do *and* you cook." She clucked her tongue, shook her head, leaned one shoulder against the wall at the kitchen entrance. "How lucky can a girl get?"

"You think this is good," he said, nodding to the pasta he dumped from colander to serving bowl, "wait till I get you in bed."

Honestly? She thought she'd die from that particular wait.

But telling him that was not the way to keep him in line—something she'd decided she was going to have to do for this affair to work. He was just this close to being too sure of himself—and of her.

She rubbed her hands up and down her arms. "I'm assuming I have you to thank for the cool air as well as for dinner?"

He moved back to the stove, stirred the simmering alfredo. "I like it cool when I cook."

She pushed off the doorway and walked farther into the kitchen, opening the refrigerator for salad makings—the least she could do to help.

What she found was a huge serving bowl of mixed greens already prepared.

"Is there anything you haven't thought of?" she asked, closing the door to the fridge.

He gave her a look that made it quite clear that he always thought of everything.

That realization and the responding twist tightening her tummy sent her out of the kitchen proper to the seat in the attached eating nook.

He'd obviously opened the bottle of wine sitting on the table there in anticipation of her arrival, and before she managed to pick it up, he was filling her glass.

That done, he brought over the single serving bowl of salad tossed with vinaigrette and another covered dish of the alfredo sauce and pasta.

Then he made a "get up" motion with his hand.

She did, holding on to her wineglass as she slid out of the seat. He moved to take her spot on the padded bench then patted his lap. "Let's eat."

Oh, my. If the idea of being that close didn't stir more than her hunger for food. She doubted she'd even be able to eat; then again, she *was* starving.

In the end, she had no trouble hiking her straight skirt up her thighs enough to straddle his.

He was hard beneath her, his belly, his legs, as was the edge of the table in the small of her back when she reached for his drink. She handed it to him before she picked up the bowl of salad and the single fork he'd supplied.

Balanced with her bottom on his knees, her calves hugging his thighs, she stabbed the salad until the tines were filled and offered him the first bite.

His eyes never left hers as he chewed, as he swallowed, as he chased the salad with a swallow of wine.

She sat with the fork hovering over the bowl she held, staring at the motions of his mouth, remembering the texture and pressure of his lips, reliving their kiss, growing wet, wondering if he noticed.

She didn't know what to do. Silly, really. She should

feed him. Or feed herself, she mused, dropping her gaze to the contents of the bowl and breathing deeply as she ate.

And then as he set his glass on the table to work open the buttons on her blouse, her breathing stopped completely. She could no longer chew or swallow, and her hands trembled, holding on to the fork and the bowl.

His fingers were fabulously talented, never fumbling as he slipped the tiny ivory-colored buttons through their holes. He bared the camisole she wore, then took the bowl and fork from her hands to pull her arms free of her sleeves.

The blouse fell loose behind her. And while her hands were free, he went ahead and pulled off the undergarment, leaving her in only her bra. That done, he reached for the bowl of pasta.

"My turn," he said, forking up a bite and offering it to her.

"Oh, no," she said before she ate. "It's mine."

Her mouth full, she did all her talking with her hands, finishing what he'd started when he'd loosened his tie, pulling the length of fine silk from his collar and sliding it through her hands, turning her mind to the wicked fun she could have with him were he tied down.

He fed her another bite, and she pondered further, thinking of binding his wrists to her headboard. Or, better yet, to the arms of the chaise lounge in her sitting room, his ankles to the legs, his knees spread wide as he straddled the seat, hers opened as she straddled him....

One of his brows lifted, his gaze moving from the tie in her hands to her eyes. "I won't be able to feed you, you know."

Mind reader. "I'm actually quite full," she managed to say, a miracle when she could barely breathe. This feeding and eating and waiting—all serving as foreplay—had her skin sizzling.

"After a couple of bites of salad and two or three of pasta?" He took another while she pulled his shirttails from his waistband and parted the shirt's front plackets. "Based on last night, I figured you for having hearty appetites."

"I do," she said, accepting the forkful of pasta he offered with a groan of dual appreciation as she threaded her fingers through the thatch of hair in the center of his chest. "Mmm."

"Is that for the food or for me?" he asked, glancing from her face to her hands.

"Both," she said, telling the truth. She massaged his pectoral muscles with the heels of her palms, slid her fingers up to cup the balls of his shoulders and squeezed. "Let me guess. A home gym."

"An employee gym, actually. Once I'm through the front door at home, I'm a vegetable."

His admission caused her to chuckle. "Couch potato?"

"ESPN twenty-four/seven," he said with a wink.

"I can see it…." And with the way he was built, she could totally imagine him being a jock. "Though my first guess would've been Bloomberg Television."

"That runs all day at the office."

She laughed again, shook her head, enjoying his quick replies far more than she should. "Men are so predictable."

"And women aren't?"

She frowned. "How have I been predictable?"

He stirred the fork through the pasta. "Your invitation promised a lot of hot sweaty action, and I haven't seen it."

"And now you won't," she teased. "You fixed the air conditioner."

He glanced up sharply. "I can break it again."

"Spending money as if it's nothing." She held off clucking her tongue.

"No," he said and grew solemn. "As if it's everything."

She thought of his clothes and his car, his cash purchase of his town house.

Then she thought of last night's wine, this night's dinner. Those didn't ring any warning bells the way his having her air conditioner put to rights did. Loudly.

There was something here she was missing. Something she was certain she needed to know. "You need to give me the bill for the repair work so I can reimburse you."

He didn't nod. He didn't shake his head. What he did was sit forward and place the bowl of food on the table. Then he hooked an elbow around her neck and pulled her mouth to his.

The kiss came out of nowhere, and she was slow to respond, to react. Her mind was back on the repairman's bill; she needed time to catch up.

But when Randy's fingers moved to the center of her back and released the hooks of her bra, catching up wasn't the issue that keeping up was.

His mouth was hard and demanding, and his fingers were as deft as his tongue. Her bra fell away from her breasts, the straps sliding down to her elbows. Randy pulled her close, crushing her chest to his.

She wrapped her arms around his neck and followed

his lead. Oh, but he felt so good, the way he held her, kissed her, the way he used his hand in the middle of her back to guide her body where he wanted.

When he pulled his mouth away, she shivered, stunned by the strength of the sensations of his lips on her jaw, her neck, his teeth tugging on her earlobe, nipping her throat.

She whimpered, and he groaned in response, moving lower to take a nipple into his mouth. He teethed and sucked, adjusting the strength and the pressure, kneading the surrounding flesh as he did.

She held his head, closed her eyes, disappeared into that place that was all about what he made her feel. What no man before had made her feel. And wasn't *that* an unexpected realization?

So much about him amazed her. The way he took charge. The way he never asked permission. The way he turned their encounter into a fantasy of surrender.

Oh, but she needed this. Someone strong enough and skilled enough, a man confident and thoughtful enough that she found the idea of letting go a thrill instead of a scare.

And so she let go, hiking her skirt up around her hips and tossing her bra to the floor, propping her elbows on the table behind her and leaning back.

Randy continued kissing her breasts and her belly, finally looking up and catching her gaze, his thick lashes heavy over his eyes that were bright with arousal.

And then he grinned a wicked wolf's grin, and settled his hands at her waist.

"On the table," was all he said before he lifted her up to sit on the edge. He hooked her knees over his forearms, spread them wide and reached between her thighs to pull aside the crotch of her panties.

He stroked her there, and she shivered, curling her toes and staring as he studied what he'd uncovered.

And then both of his hands were beneath her skirt, his thumbs stroking the bare flesh plumped up on either side of the entrance to her sex. She closed her eyes and whimpered.

"Feels good?"

"You can't imagine." This was what she loved about being female, this anticipation, this build-up, the burst of sensation to come.

"How's this?" he asked, leaning in to cover her with his mouth.

He ran his tongue through her folds and she gasped, holding on to the table's edge and praying she didn't crash with the furniture in a heap to the floor.

Whether it was the thrill of the situation—sex with a man she didn't even know, one she couldn't escape or walk away from when they lived right next door—or his skill and technique didn't matter.

She had never in her life felt what she was feeling now. The physical rush unnerved her, left her shaking and unable to open her eyes. But there was so much more than sex going on here. And that was the truth of the fear. She was beyond being able to think.

It was all she could do to deal with what she was feeling, with what Randy's fingers were doing, with where he had his tongue, with how he played and tasted and kissed her with his lips.

Her moan drowned out the hum of the refrigerator and the ring of her cell phone tucked into her purse. Randy pulled back, and she wanted to hit him for leaving her wanting.

"I'm not answering that," she said breathlessly.

He chuckled, and she heard him shuffling around on the seat. "I hope not."

"Then ignore the distraction and get back to work," she said, and he laughed, the sound rolling up from his gut to his throat.

He finished adjusting and squirming and reached for both of her hands, pulling her up to sit on the table's edge. The rush of blood from her head left her dizzy; it took her several seconds to open her eyes.

When she did, she realized he was erect and sheathed and waiting for her to sit in his lap. A deep breath, a long slow exhalation, and she did, easing from the table onto her knees and bracing them on either side of his thighs.

Then, her gaze on his, she reached between her legs and guided him exactly where she needed him to be, lowering her body slowly, taking him in, breathing sharply as he filled her.

Oh, but it was hard not to look away, to remain so intimately, visually bonded when it was more than their bodies involved.

There was a deeper connection here, the same one with which she'd been hit on the balcony last night. She knew it even while she forced it aside to enjoy the physical bliss.

Her fingers gripping his shoulders, she leaned forward and used that support as well as her knees to ride, grinding her hips, rotating slowly, pressing the heels of her palms into the muscles of his shoulders that bunched as he tightened his hold on her waist.

His head dropped back, his eyes closed. He guided her exactly as he wanted her, stroked up as she slid down. Lips parted, she caught her tongue between her teeth and watched the tight set of his jaw, the pulse that popped there, the sweat that beaded and fell.

Men were supposed to be the visual creatures, but the sight of Randy struggling for control sent her own into a spiraling loss. She gripped him harder with her hands and her sex, and then she let go, shuddering, dying, coming apart.

He followed, a hard upward surge that knocked the table and sent the bowl of salad skittering over the floor. When he groaned, she felt the vibrations there where their bodies were joined.

And when he finished, the shiver that ran through him shook loose the wrapping with which she'd carefully packaged her heart.

4

"So? Did he break your heart or not?"

Randy lay on top of Claire in her bed, his elbows on either side of her shoulders supporting his weight. He tangled his fingers into the loose ends of her hair where the strands lay draped on the pillow.

"Why are you bringing that up again now? It hardly seems the time to talk about another man." Her voice was breathless, her fingers digging into his backside and pulling his body further into hers.

He grit his teeth, settled more deeply between her legs, let his mind drift with intent. Her query and observation were valid. Why he would insist on bringing up their bargain instead of lying back and enjoying her body?

The reason was simple.

The two were inextricably linked.

He wouldn't be here if she hadn't agreed to the give and take. And he needed the give and take to secure her as he did all his possessions.

"It only takes a yes or a no."

"Sure. If I were a man."

"Really," he said and rolled away onto one elbow, staring down into her face. "This coming from the same woman who demanded no strings."

She looked at him, her wide-eyed gaze clearly accusing him of losing his mind. "With you. That doesn't mean there haven't been strings in my past."

"But you've cut them since."

"I'm here, aren't I?"

She was, yes. But that didn't answer the question. He spread out his hand over her belly. "You are, and you agreed to answer my question."

She huffed, pulled the sheet up to cover her breasts. "And they say women use sex as a bargaining tool."

"Is that what I'm doing?"

"What would you call it?"

Survival. Getting what he wanted. Same thing he'd been doing for more than half of his life. "Waiting."

"For what?" She moved her legs, tangled her feet with his. "I already sent you an invitation."

"To catch my breath," he admitted without thinking, and to which she could only reply, "Oh."

After that lapse, making her aware of his weakness, of how close he was to losing control, he remained silent and unmoving, even when she placed her hand on top of his.

"Okay then," she said, blowing out a long, slow breath. "His name was Wayne. And he did. We were in high school. He was out of my league. I let myself fall in love when I knew better."

Randy smiled to himself. He loved that she felt as if she owed him more of an explanation than he wanted. "Yes or no was all I asked for."

She shook her head on the pillow. "I can't reduce that relationship to one word."

So, she hadn't let it go? "Why not?"

"Because it was a turning point. Because it taught me so much."

"Such as?"

Laughing softly, she shifted onto her side to face him. "I can't believe you want to talk. Men don't talk."

About themselves, no. But that's not what this was. "I can stop."

"Oh, no. Please don't." She laughed again. It was a husky, throaty sound that worked its way into his gut. "I just thought you might have caught your breath by now."

He wasn't sure he was going to. He was still rock hard. Yet, he was here for more than the sex—a fact he was determined to make her understand—even if sex had been the original intent of the card she'd slipped through his door.

He moved his hand higher, covered and massaged one of her breasts. "We have all night, Claire."

"I can't get used to hearing you say my name," she said with a shiver and sigh. "It's like I know you, but don't know you."

"Do you want to know me?"

She tugged on his chest hair with one hand, on the hair growing low on his belly with the fingers of the other. "Had you asked me yesterday, I don't think I'd have given you the same answer."

"Is that a yes?"

"Yes," she softly.

He felt her exhalation of breath like a tickling flutter. "Are you afraid I'll break your heart?"

She hesitated—he wondered if he'd pushed too far—before responding. "If you do, it will be my own fault for not sticking to the invitation's no strings and no questions."

He slid his hand up to her shoulder, pushed her to her back, climbed over her. "We never talked about the strings."

"You're right," she said, opening her legs as he moved between. "We didn't. Should we?"

He used her moisture to ease his way, pushing inside to fill her. "I think it's too late."

CLAIRE TRULY couldn't remember the last time she'd slept with a man. Not the last time she'd had sex—that memory was quite clear—but the last time she'd closed her eyes and fallen asleep with a man's arms wrapped around her.

Even tonight she hadn't slept long, no more than two hours she guessed, having glanced at the bedside clock after she and Randy had climbed the town house stairs.

Once they'd tumbled into bed, she'd lost all track of time.

What she hadn't lost even while sleeping was the awareness that they'd discussed the question he'd asked of her, yet hadn't brought up her question to him.

He couldn't be blamed, she supposed. She would never have responded to his without prodding.

It was time to do a little prodding of her own.

Randy lay spooned up behind her, his arm draped over her waist, his breathing deep and even. She turned onto her stomach, sidled closer and trailed tiny kisses over his collarbone.

He smelled warm and clean; he tasted alive. He felt as if he belonged between her cool cotton sheets for more than one night, and that left her shaken because this was supposed to be a no-strings-attached fling.

When she finally looked up, she found his eyes wide open, his lashes thick and sweeping. For several seconds, she remained still, catching her breath that he'd stolen, measuring the hard beats of both of their hearts.

Then, pushing onto her hands and knees, she crawled over his body and stared down. "My turn."

"Be my guest," he said, rolling onto his back, his hands at her hips settling her over his groin. His penis stirred between her spread thighs.

"I wasn't talking about sex," she said, eyes narrowed. "It's time to talk."

He fought a grin. "We talked already."

"I talked. I answered your question." She leaned forward, braced her hands on his shoulders. "Now you answer mine."

"Okay." He nodded where he lay on the pillow, reached up with one hand to toy with the ends of her hair. "Nothing."

She flexed her fingers into the muscles of his shoulders. "Nothing what?"

"You asked me what I was hiding behind my sports car and designer suits. I answered nothing."

She didn't believe him. She knew image. She knew disguises. It was her business, after all.

She also knew all about hiding. She didn't talk about it, but she knew. "The car doesn't fit. That's a response to a midlife crisis, not a way to get around town."

He rubbed the thumb of his other hand over her hipbone, his penis growing thick. "It gets the job done."

"As does my Camry," she countered, hating the creeping distraction of sex.

"You're not a believer in 'if you've got it, flaunt it'?"

"No. But neither are you."

"You sure you know me that well?"

Strangely enough, she was. "I know that you're too comfortable in your own skin to show off."

"I don't need to. I let the clothes do it for me."

She growled down. "You are so full of it."

"That makes the wrong one of us," he said, sliding one of her hands away from his shoulder and down the center of his body to his cock.

She wrapped him in her fingers, stroked him, squeezed him. "That's all I'm going to get?"

He surged into her hand. "I haven't had complaints before."

"I wasn't talking about your equipment." And selfishly she didn't like thinking about the women he'd had before. "I was talking about you not answering my question. I answered yours."

"I gave you an answer."

"It was evasive and circular and hardly forthcoming," she said, teasing though honest. When he remained silent, she added, "I told you about Wayne."

"I knew a Wayne when I was younger." His fingers flexed on her thighs. "He ran the soup kitchen where I ate a lot of my meals."

Her hand stilled, as did her whole body. "Why did you eat in soup kitchens?"

"Because the couple who adopted me didn't just take me in." His expression grew chilled. "They made sure I understood where I had come from and where I would end up if I didn't pay attention."

"Pay attention to what?" she asked, her broken voice barely recognizable. *Where in the world had he come from?*

"To the fact that money does buy happiness."

No. She wasn't buying it. "You can't believe that."

"I've never been happier in my life."

"But not because of money."

"Sure. Money buys me the designer suits and the sports car."

She slid off his thighs to sit cross-legged beside him. "So, your happiness is dependent on what you own."

He hesitated a moment, stacking his hands beneath his head. "Not so much on what I own as on knowing that I don't have to do without."

It wasn't hard to understand the sentiment. Having money made a lot of life easier to deal with. But money buying happiness?

She started to tell him that doing without was hardly the end of the world. But she stopped because she wouldn't know a thing about it.

She'd never missed a meal she didn't need to miss. Her survival had never been tied to the generosity of others. Randy's obviously had.

And he'd responded by guaranteeing, like Scarlet, that he would never go hungry again.

Claire reached over and smoothed her hand from his elbow to his hip. "What one thing do you most want to buy but haven't?"

"For someone who went into this arrangement insisting on no questions, you've certainly changed your tune," he said, his voice gruff, his breathing harsh, his erection swelling with her lingering touch.

He was right—and she deserved every bit of the blame. She'd only wanted a fling; how could she have known he'd be so intriguing? Or that she'd want to dig for all of the truths he hid?

Right now what she wanted was to let the questions go. To stop talking. To get back to the reason they were here.

"Why don't you think on that and answer me tomorrow?" she said, getting up to her hands and knees and crawling between his legs.

He spread them wider. "Sounds like a hell of a plan."

Smiling, she ringed her fingers beneath the head of his cock and took him into her mouth. He let her know of his pleasure with the sounds he made, grunts and groans and strangled gasps.

Then he let her know he'd had enough. He pushed her away, rolled on a condom, and urged her to climb on top. He didn't have to urge much at all.

She returned to straddling his hips and took him in her hand, lifting up and guiding him to her center. He filled her completely, perfectly, as if in some weird twist of fate she'd found the man with the body most suited to hers.

It made no sense. There was no such thing.

Yet she couldn't push away the memory of catching his gaze on the balcony. Of the connection, the sense that he was the only man she needed.

He held her by the hips. She leaned forward, her hands on his chest where she braced her weight as she rode. She took her time. She wanted to enjoy the tingling pressure, the sweet unbearable ache, the feel of Randy forever.

Forever took no time in coming, and neither did she. Even after telling herself to wait, all it took was his fingers sliding from her hip to the sweet spot where her body had taken his in.

He stroked her, teased her, wet his finger with her moisture and played with her clit. She shuddered and searched for the edge of her control.

What she found was the freedom of surrender. She gave up, crying out as she came, feeling the surge of Randy's release deep inside as he followed.

It was quick and reckless, a heated burst that wasn't enough. It was the fling she'd asked for, but as she curled up beneath the sheets next to his big warm body, she decided that Santa hadn't quite got it right.

GOOD THING Claire hadn't gone into this affair expecting true romance—or even breakfast in bed. Randy was gone when she woke. She showered and dressed for the office.

Had she known when she left last night that she'd arrive home to a working AC, she would've packed up her laptop and carted her work home with her.

A day spent in slouchy sweats sounded like heaven. But she hadn't known, making pumps and panty hose the order of the day.

Before she headed for her car, however, she headed for Café Eros. Calories, schmalories. After last night, she needed caffeine and sugar, and no one provided both better than Chloe Matthews.

At the entrance to the alley leading out of Court du Chaud, Claire ran—not unexpectedly—into Perry Brazille. Perry wore an orange tank top with her gauzy ankle-length skirt. "This is a cruel, cruel joke. If I wanted to sunbathe in winter, I'd live Down Under."

"No kidding," Claire said. "I'm hoping coffee and Chloe's Christmas pastries will go a long way to reminding me that Santa's on his way."

Perry hooked her arm through Claire's. "I'm right there with you, though I was thinking of starting the day with chocolate."

Laughing, the two women entered the café's courtyard where seasonal blooms spilled in a riot of color from the center fountain that now served as a planter. They chose a nearby table covered in a cloth of Christmas red and gave their order to the server.

"How's Della?" Claire asked, knowing Perry had been spending as many nights at her aunt's place lately as at her own.

Perry gave a noncommittal shrug. "She's not eating, hardly sleeping. Is wasting away to nothing."

Della Brazille was a prominent New Orleans psychic whose services were often sought by the NOPD. While Perry kept her aunt's confidences, she wasn't always as successful at hiding her own concern for the toll taken by Della's mental gift.

The server brought their order, and Claire poured cream into her coffee. "I figured things were rough since you haven't been home much lately."

Perry remained quiet, sipping at her own coffee—strong and straight black—before her mouth broke into a grin. "She has a suitor. A detective. She's being stubborn about his advances, of course."

"Why?"

"Who knows? I think he scares her. Not in a bad way. Just in a...man way."

"Now that's something to which I can totally relate." Claire sliced into her warm apple fritter. "Have you ever had a man try to buy you?"

"Buy me how? Pay me to sleep with him?" Perry asked.

That wasn't what Claire had thought was happening; she certainly hoped she hadn't been wrong. "More like to be with him."

Perry cradled her mug in both hands. "Without sex."

"No." Claire shook her head. "There's sex, but there's also talking and cooking and dating and air-conditioner repairs involved."

"Sounds like domestic bliss to me," Perry said, biting into her chocolate cruller.

It was edging toward exactly that when it was supposed to be a holiday fling. Claire sighed. "It's got to be the heat. I didn't get my Christmas cards mailed out when I should have. I haven't shopped for a thing. And then I thought it would be fun to spend the holidays with a man—"

"So you bought one."

Was that what she'd done? Bought Randy with the promise of sex? "Not really. I put him on my list and Santa brought him early."

"And now you're thinking you might be ringing in the New Year with wedding bells?"

"Oh good grief, no." Making the leap from a fling to marriage would require legs a lot longer than hers. "I'm just being forced to accept that I'm not cut out for a meaningless fling."

"Welcome to the club, girlfriend."

"How do men manage it?"

"I like to pretend they don't. That they agonize and suffer like we do." Perry grinned as she reached for the last bite of her cruller. "But since they don't have girlfriends to bond with, they keep it all inside where it gets toxic and deadly."

"Hmm. I wondered what caused all that yelling at the TV during sporting events."

"That. And then there's the smell."

Claire sputtered her coffee. "There's definitely something to be said for not having to share a bathroom."

"You can say that again."

5

RANDY STOOD staring out his fourth-floor office window at the tops of the palms edging the sidewalk below. On his desk lay the marketing portfolio for the image-consulting firm who'd be tackling the offices of the Flatbacker Foundation.

First Impressions. Owner, Claire Braden.

The spiel he'd given the partners about the office needing a makeover and the foundation a corporate image—not to mention a working environment—more in keeping with their mission statement was a load of bull.

He'd needed an in with Claire.

He'd wanted her from the moment he'd first seen her on her balcony. He'd been determined to take his time, to discover what he could about her before making a move. The approach was the same one he'd used for years when pursuing an acquisition, when engaged in a power play.

But now that he'd met her, slept with her, gotten to know more about her than he'd expected to learn so easily or soon, what had seemed a cut-and-dried plan had him second-guessing the tenets that had been the backbone of his success.

Until moving to New Orleans in September at his uncle's request, he'd lived in Texas—Austin, to be exact—

where his first twelve years were the ones that held the most memories.

Memories of a life in foster care and months spent on the streets before Charles and Elizabeth Schneider stepped into his path of self-destruction and saved him from himself.

His adoptive parents had provided a fair upbringing in which sentiment played no part. What they'd taught him instead was the value of loyalty, the return gained by respect, the worth of a portfolio.

He'd come to the Schneider's with the clothes on his back, clothes that had gone up in smoke literally leaving him with nothing to his name, nothing of his own, nothing but twelve years he wished he could forget.

Sounds of sirens and despair. Sights of flashing lights and desperation. Smells that came in one of three fragrances: soured or spoiled or stale.

He grit his teeth against the rise of emotion that churned and burned center chest. Those memories were ones no man—or woman—could take away.

Or so he'd thought until meeting Claire.

She was aggressive. She was confident. She knew what she wanted and went after it. And she seemed to want him. It was almost as if she was the piece of his life he'd never accepted was missing.

She'd asked him what one thing he most wanted had he not yet been able to buy. The answer was simple.

He wanted Claire.

CLAIRE DIDN'T HEAR from Randy all day. She hadn't told him where she worked or given him her cell or office number. She figured with his resources, he'd have no trouble finding her if that was what he wanted.

Obviously, it wasn't.

That reality should have come as a relief. If he'd changed his mind about hooking up, she wouldn't have to answer the question he'd asked her last night before leaving. Of course, she wouldn't be getting an answer to hers either.

But somehow she couldn't equate his tales of acquiring material possessions with her having to choose between being a kept woman and living in poverty without telling him why.

She'd never had to do without, at least not in the sense that he had. Her family had been very average, very middle class. If she'd had to give up anything, it had been the friends she'd left behind with her family's every move.

In those cases, having money wouldn't have made a bit of difference. Starting over was an emotional—not a financial—burden. What the constant moves had done, however, was make her hyperaware of what she had to do to fit in.

Switch out boots and jeans for flippy skirts and ballerina flats. Wear big bangs and big curls one year, a sharply wedged pageboy the next. Dump the Goth-look when sweaters and polos and boat shoes became the order of the day.

She'd made a career out of image, the downside being that she'd never taken time to discover herself. Even now she dressed to meet a client's expectations rather than cementing a look that simply said, "Claire."

Pulling her Camry into the garage, she briefly wondered if Randy was already home. She'd left the office earlier than usual; in the morning she had her first meeting with the partners of the Flatbacker Foundation, and she needed a good night's sleep.

She walked through the living room toward the stairs, kicking off her shoes, peeling off her panty hose, tossing her purse and attaché to the sofa. And then she laughed. That habit right there pretty much defined who she was.

Wondering how seriously her clients would take image advice from a world-class slob, she walked from her bedroom onto the balcony to take in the Christmas tree, doing a double-take as she registered Randy slouched back and relaxing in one of the wrought iron chairs.

Once she'd caught her breath, she glared and said, "Two days, and I've figured out two important things about you."

His mouth curled deviously. "Which are?"

"You don't like discussion questions." She held up one finger then another. "And you know too much about breaking and entering."

"I'm better with numbers than words." He paused, added, "And even better at picking locks."

She moved to the opposite corner of the balcony and leaned her back against the brick wall. The position afforded her a view of Randy to her right, the courtyard to her left.

One view to calm her. One to undo every bit of that calm. Her smile felt shaky when she responded. "A man of convenient and marketable skills."

He laughed. "I'll give you the CPA. I'm not so sure my days as a delinquent would inspire employer confidence."

As an image consultant with no image, she could relate. Her gaze settled on Randy's laced fingers where they rested at his waist, and she swallowed hard. "So your ability to buy happiness is a result of crunching numbers?"

He gave a brief shrug. "I was a day-trader for a few years. Got out before it became a health hazard."

"Someone made you an offer you couldn't refuse?"

"My uncle." He shifted in his chair and stretched out his legs. "He and his partners were about to conservatively administer themselves into bankruptcy."

"Ouch," she said, his words ringing a faraway bell. "I'm sure your obsession with the almighty dollar will pay off for them nicely."

"What about you?" he asked, seeming to settle in even more comfortably.

She, on the other hand, felt as stiff as if she were awaiting a root canal. "What about me?"

"A life of poverty, or that of a kept woman?"

Oh. *That.* She glanced toward the tree and gathered her wits before looking back. "I'll answer, but I want you to know it's not a fair question."

One of his dark brows lifted. "Was 'fair' part of our bargain?"

"No, but this question is the sort that deserves more than a one- or two-word answer."

"One or two words are all that I want."

"Why?" When his lips narrowed, she went on, no matter her aggravation. "At least tell me why you don't want an explanation."

This time his shrug was careless. "I don't need one. The explanation is inherent in the answer."

Not for her, it wasn't. "It's not inherent. It's complicated."

He nodded; she couldn't decide if it was being thoughtful or condescending. "You want me to know that choosing to live as a kept woman would give you the means to help others. That it wouldn't be about what you might want for yourself."

Uncanny how accurate he was. Was he testing her? Deciding how they fit out of bed? If she shared his appreciation for the finer things in life?

If she understood the happiness of not doing without what money was able to buy?

"Yes. I would choose to be a kept woman."

"For the reasons I gave?"

Infuriating man. "I thought you didn't need an explanation."

"I don't. You do."

She wanted to roll her eyes. He was obviously out to prove that being a *have* was better than being a *have not*, that there was nothing wrong with enjoying the fruits of one's labors. And there wasn't.

But equating riches to emotional well-being wasn't the same. At least not for her. The things she wanted most out of life were things that couldn't be bought—no matter what personal wealth she acquired.

She wondered if their priorities were truly that far apart. Or if he simply took a perverse pleasure in goading her. For some reason, she wanted to bet on the latter. "What I need is an explanation from you."

"About?"

Her turn to make him squirm. "What one thing do you want most in life that you haven't yet acquired?"

He didn't hesitate or stutter or make her beg. All he did was meet her gaze and say, "You."

HE'D WONDERED if she would answer. No, he'd wondered if she would answer honestly. If she'd choose to be noble or if she'd put herself out there and let the chips fall. Hell, he wouldn't have challenged her if he'd thought all she would do was cave.

He could've argued her choice proved his point that happiness was most definitely for sale—even if her happiness seemed bound up with having the means to help others. But he hadn't. He'd given her a noble out. One she'd refused.

Then he'd pushed out of the chair where he'd been sitting, taken hold of her wrist, and tugged her into the bedroom. He was tired of talking. The sex they'd shared last night had been like a series of flash fires exploding, but with too much conversation between.

Tonight would be all about making love.

He wanted to drink her in, to learn her, to make himself so much a part of her she'd lose where she ended and he began. And he wasn't deterred by the fact that what he was describing sounded like emotional involvement.

That's not what it was. It couldn't be. He wouldn't let that happen.

Standing at the foot of her bed, he faced her to unbutton her soft pink blouse. Her skirt was brown with pinstripes to match. She worked for herself, didn't see clients every day, yet she dressed like a corporate lawyer.

She took her business seriously, as did he, and that pleased him. He would never have to explain work keeping him late at the office. He wouldn't demand she reschedule an appointment that conflicted with his plans.

They fit together. They worked. They were the closest thing to being a matched two-of-a-kind he'd known. Except for their disparate viewpoints on money.

And though he was in no mood to talk, he couldn't let

the subject go. "I'm not a bad guy, Claire. But I don't like having to defend my life."

She glanced from his fingers on her buttons up to his face. Her eyes were a misty blue. "You want to talk about your life while you're taking off my clothes?"

"Yes." He peeled her blouse off her shoulders, tugged it from the waistband of her skirt. Then he reached up to loosen her hair from its binding. "You're a part of it now."

"I am?" she asked, her eyes drifting shut as he finger-combed the long strands.

His gut tightened. "I may be a bastard when it comes to money. But I don't shag and run."

She smiled at that, a soft lift of the same lips he wanted to feel kissing his body. "You were gone when I woke up this morning."

"I stayed as long as I could." He thought of her spooned up against him and tugged down her skirt's zipper. The garment slid to the floor. "I had a breakfast meeting."

"Mmm. I'm starving." She stood there barefoot wearing only her bra and panties. Gooseflesh pebbled her skin. "I haven't eaten much of anything the last two days."

"Breakfast in bed. I promise." He released the clasp of her bra, then filled his hands with the weight of her breasts. Her nipples grew hard in his palms.

"Scrambled eggs and bacon and buttered toast and orange juice, please." She grabbed his wrists, wet her lips with her tongue, opened her eyes and met his gaze. "Mmm. You make me hungry."

He couldn't even speak. His throat had shut down. It was all he could do to release his belt buckle, toe off his shoes and shuck down his pants.

Claire took care of his shirt and tie, and then there was

nothing between them but the cotton of his boxer briefs and the scrap of silk she wore as panties. He quickly skinned them out of both. She brought up her arms to wrap around his neck and urged his mouth to hers.

He kissed her. Stroking his hands down her sides, he pushed her back to the bed. She was warm and giving beneath him, making it hard to remember this was not about involvement but convenience, compatibility, companionship.

He kissed his way down the center of her body, lingering in the dip of her throat, feeling her shudder when he nuzzled her there. Her scent was light, clean skin and shampoo. His mouth drifted to her breast.

She arched up into his body and moaned. "I like the way you feed me."

He groaned against her skin, moved to her other breast and sucked, rolling her nipple with his tongue before letting go and trailing his kisses lower.

She shivered, flexed her fingers into the fabric of the quilt beneath her, whimpered when he pushed her heels to her hips and settled between the V of her legs.

The skin of her belly was sweet-tasting and smooth, as was that of her thighs. What he wanted was more light by which to see her, but it had grown dark outside and the bedroom closed around them like a cocoon.

He breathed deeply of her sex, the musky warmth, salty and moist and aroused, then slipped his tongue between her folds to circle her clit.

Her cries grew louder, and she begged for more with an upward surge of her hips. He tongued the hard knot of nerves, her plump flesh, circled her entrance and pushed inside. She sucked in a sharp breath, and then began to pant.

His cock throbbed. He ached to fill her. The need worsened when she begged, "Randy, please."

Another time, another place…another woman and he would have waited. With Claire, his desire was too strong.

Braced on his knees, he rolled on a condom before bringing his body to rest above hers. The absence of light in the room didn't keep her eyes from sparkling.

She reached between them, held his cock, rubbed the head in and out and around her sex, finally pushing up to take him deep into her body.

He settled in, amazed at how they fit together, at how little control he had when buried inside where she was so tight and so warm.

Her hands squeezed his shoulders. Her heels dug into the backs of his thighs. She moved up and down to the beat of her need, holding him harder, pushing against him. He clenched his jaw until he swore his molars would crack.

And then it was too late. Holding back wasn't going to happen. He stroked long and hard and fast, and then he let go, sliding a hand between them, fingering her clit.

She followed, crying out as she came. The sounds she made, the touch of her hands, the way she'd asked him for nothing nearly tore him apart. That didn't mean this was emotional involvement.

That's not what it was. It couldn't be. He wouldn't let that happen.

HE STAYED THE NIGHT.

She couldn't believe it, couldn't believe either that she was the first into the shower, or that he was still in her bed when she came out of the bathroom wearing her robe.

She would have loved to shower with him, to get her hands on his warm, wet and nicely large body, to soap him up and stroke him, to wrap her legs around his waist as he backed her into the wall and filled her.

But she didn't have time this morning for that pleasure. Her appointment was scheduled for nine.

She was in the kitchen pouring coffee when Randy walked up behind her. He'd showered, but he hadn't shaved. And she had to admit she liked the look of the day's growth of beard.

She wasn't as crazy about the feel, however; it scratched when he bent and kissed her.

"We're going to have to talk about your face," she said, turning to pour his coffee. "If you want to kiss me on a regular basis, the stubble's got to go."

"I'll get rid of it tonight." He took the coffee she offered. "I'm late, and need to run home and change."

Sipping her coffee, she nodded, thinking how easily she could get used to this morning routine. "You still owe me breakfast in bed."

He grinned, his teeth so white in contrast to his lashes and beard. "Tomorrow. I promise. You'll need a good start to the day."

Always Mr. Cryptic. She tried not to sound too interested when she asked, "Why's that?"

"I have a fund-raising Christmas gala for work tomorrow night. It's at the Bourbon Orleans." He paused, one heartbeat, two. "I'd be honored if you'd accompany me."

At the last minute? He was asking her to a big-time social event at the last minute? "As your date?"

"Well, yeah." His grin broke her resolve not to fall for him hard. "I already have a limo driver."

She rolled her eyes, silently panicking over what she would wear. "In that case, I'd love to."

"Great. We'll need to leave here at six-thirty."

"I think I can manage," she said, and brought her cup to her mouth.

He started for the door, stopped. "Do you want me to wait for you? You can follow me downtown if you want."

Follow him? Downtown? Why? She'd lived here longer than he had. "I think I can manage."

"Okay, then." He left his coffee cup in the sink and bussed her cheek with a kiss. "I'll see you there."

"See me where?" she asked, the niggling of the night before suddenly returning.

"At the office," he said, and left her with a wink on his way out the door.

The office. *The office.* The one where his uncle "conservatively administered" educational grants and scholarship funds. She collapsed onto the bench of the breakfast nook.

She was sleeping with a client. Er, a prospective client. Either way, could she possibly be any more unprofessional?

Not only that, she'd agreed to be his date at a work function tomorrow night. Talk about conflict of interest.

And now she was going to have to walk into this morning's meeting and pretend all was right in her very screwed up world.

This called for more than a stop at Café Eros, she mused, rubbing her aching forehead. This called for a full-fledged therapy session.

Claire found her purse on the sofa where she'd left it last night, dug her phone from inside, curled into the sofa's cushy corner, and dialed Tess Autrey's private line.

"Ooh. A New Orleans area code. This could only be the fabulous Claire Braden," Tess said when she came on the line. "What's up?"

It was all Claire could do to squeak out, "Help!"

6

CLAIRE PARKED her car, checked her reflection in the visor's mirror, grabbed her purse and the leather binder from her attaché, and headed for the building.

It was eight-fifty-five.

Tess had been right. There was nothing Claire could do this morning beyond going about her job in the most professional way possible and dealing with Randy later. Unfortunately, dealing with Randy meant dealing with her heart.

And keeping her heart out of this meeting—not to mention her pique and other assorted murderous emotions—was going to require skills she wasn't sure she had in her personal image portfolio.

She took a deep breath, hit the elevator call button, wondering why she was even going through this charade. She didn't believe for a minute that she'd leave here having landed the Flatbacker account. This was Randy's handiwork.

He'd seen her, he'd wanted her and he'd done what life had taught him to do. He'd ponied up the bucks and bought her.

She didn't want to believe it but how could she not when his actions screamed louder than words? Never in her life had she felt like such a cheap piece of meat.

The elevator car arrived, and she punched the button for the fourth floor. On the ride up, she worked for calm, smoothing down her blazer, adjusting the gold chain hanging around her neck, running a hand over her hair.

When the door opened, she took a deep breath and stepped out into a lobby that surprised her. It was exactly the look her research on the old-moneyed financial firm had led her to expect—rich wood, expensive leather and woven rugs, original oils in gilt frames.

"Damn you, Randy," she murmured under her breath. This was so going to be a waste of time.

Instead of backing out quietly the way she'd come in, Claire lifted her chin, approached the receptionist's desk and smiled at the young woman's softly spoken, "Good Morning. May I help you?"

She offered her business card. "Claire Braden. I have a nine o'clock appointment with Luther Andrews."

The receptionist checked her monitor display then gestured toward the waiting area as she picked up the phone. "I'll let him know you're here."

"Thank you." Stepping away, Claire studied the heavy furniture, the floral arrangements and low-burning lamps, the paintings depicting hunting dogs and riders on horseback hanging on the dark paneled walls.

What in the world was she doing here?

Unless the foundation's partners had decided to downplay the fact that they could well afford the philanthropy for which they had earned such high regard…

What in the world was she doing here?

Oh, wait. She was here because she'd gotten the jump on her lover, inviting him over for drinks and into her bed before he managed to acquire her the old-fashioned way. With wads and wads of cash.

"Ms. Braden."

Forcing a smile and momentarily banishing her uncharitable thoughts, she turned at the sound of the deep male voice and held out her hand. "Claire, please."

"Claire, I'm Luther." The older man spoke with a John Wayne drawl that fit the boots he wore and the western cut of his suit. His hand swallowed hers. "Let's stop by my nephew's office, pick up the boy and get this tour started, this being his idea after all."

She liked how he cut straight to the chase. She also liked hearing him call Randy a boy. That tickled her, even when she was ready to throttle him. "I must admit that after seeing the lobby, I'm wondering why I'm here."

Luther laughed, a hearty, good ol' boy guffaw. "Most people never get beyond seeing what you just saw. It's the rest of the place that my nephew wants to focus on."

Interesting, she mused, walking through the door Luther opened and into a long hallway—a hallway no less well-appointed than the lobby in the same navy, wine and deep hunter green. Their footsteps fell silently on the thick carpet.

Randy's office brought her first surprise. For one thing, he wasn't there. For another, the room couldn't have been more sterile. White walls, industrial gray carpet, metal file cabinets and a matching desk.

Only the computer equipment and ergonomic desk chair fit the image of the man she knew. It was hard to picture him working in these conditions.

Harder to admit she'd based her entire opinion of him

on the car he drove, the clothes he wore, the cash he'd paid for his town house.

She'd never even factored in the way he treated her.

How shallow could she be?

"Randy, my nephew, came to work with us in September. This was the only empty office." Luther cleared his throat as if embarrassed. "Since he's the one putting in the most hours, it only seemed right to let the boy outfit the place."

Surely the rest of the offices weren't so...spare, would be a nice word. Plain, a compliment. Randy's office was nothing if not ugly.

What else about him was there to learn? "Should we wait for him? Or do you want to show me around?"

Luther inclined his head, gestured with one hand toward the end of the hall. "Let's head on down to the O.K. Corral. Least that's what Randy calls my office. When he's not calling it a barn, anyway."

Walking at Luther's side, Claire struggled to reconcile what she'd expected with what she'd found. Admittedly, an old cowboy was the last thing she'd expected Randy's uncle to be. But then the last three days had brought little in the way of normal expectations.

"There you are," Luther was saying as Claire walked through his office door. "Straighten up here now so I can introduce you to Ms. Braden."

"Claire," she said without thinking, her brain engaged elsewhere—specifically by the sight of Randy's backside covered in fashionable gray wool.

Leaning forward to study the *Wall Street Journal,* he stood with his back to the door, his hands braced wide on Luther's desk, a platinum watchband circling one wrist.

Nine o'clock in the morning, and he'd already lost his suit coat and cuffed back his white shirtsleeves.

But oh, did he look good from behind, broad in the shoulders, lean in the hips. She couldn't help it. She thought about him naked, about the way he covered her body, sliding into her as far as he could.

He straightened and turned and walked toward her; her heart thumped so loudly she couldn't hear a word he said. He was beautiful, gorgeous—his eyes, his mouth, the way he moved. She was falling for him, and she didn't know what to do.

Luther kept her from having to do anything more than hold out her hand. "Claire Braden, my nephew, Randy Schneider. Randy, Claire's here to put your world to rights."

Put his world to rights.

Luther had no idea, Randy mused, watching Claire settle her portfolio in one arm, take up her pen in the other hand and ready herself to take notes. "I've seen her work. I have no doubt she'll do just that."

A blush washed over Claire's cheeks. She avoided his gaze and glanced around the office, moving to the pedestal in the corner that held an original Frederic Remington bronze. "I appreciate the opportunity. And my first impression would be, Luther, that you love the American West. The detail in Remington's sculptures has always amazed me."

"I spent the biggest part of my life breaking irascible horses." Behind Claire's back, Luther gave Randy a silent thumbs-up. "Leastways when the offices were still in Texas, and I could sneak away for long weekends spent at the ranch."

Claire nodded. "You haven't always been in New Orleans then?"

"No, ma'am." Luther made his way behind his desk and sank into his leather chair sized for a mammoth.

He gestured for Randy and Claire to take the visitor chairs. Claire declined. She chose, instead, to circle the office and take notes.

Luther went on. "We came over a few years back when Lionel's wife took sick and wanted to spend the rest of her time close to family out near Lake Pontchartrain."

"Lionel Burns is one of Luther's partners," Randy explained, arms crossed, a shoulder braced against the doorjamb. "His office is the next door down."

Luther leaned back in his chair, propped one boot heel on the corner of his desk. "Randy accuses Lionel of working out of a fish camp."

"Fish camp?" Pen scratching across paper, Claire turned toward Randy, lifting a brow and fighting a corresponding lift of her lips.

Such a tiny movement of her mouth and it tied his gut in knots. "Lionel's aesthetic appreciation runs toward what he calls a maritime theme."

"I see." More notes, another squashed smile. "And the third partner?"

Luther's chair squeaked as he leaned farther back. "That would be Lester Grant. He's out in the Gulf on a rig most of the time."

"When he's here, he stores his hardhats and jumpsuits and bathymetric charts in his office," Randy added, pausing while Claire's pen flew.

"Go on ahead, Randy, and show Claire around the place. Give her a better idea of what we have for her to work with." Luther waved his hand toward the door and chuckled. "She might decide to walk out and never come back."

"I doubt that will happen but, yes. I would like a tour." She crossed her arms over her binder and held it to her chest, waiting patiently while Randy processed the idea that she might actually leave.

He couldn't see it happening. She was a professional…one he'd manipulated in order to get his way. The thought brought a frisson of alarm as he said, "Then let's go."

He walked her through the remaining rooms on the floor, explaining Lionel's background in the merchant marines, Lester's in oil, and how the two had originally hooked up with Luther in Korea during that military conflict.

Once their tours of duty were over, the three had hitched their way around the world, meeting a Parisian "flatbacker" who'd convinced them there was a fortune to be made were they to import French lingerie into the States.

"Let me get this straight," Claire said, settling into a chair at the conference room table once finished with the full tour. "Your uncle and his partners got their start working with a prostitute they met in Paris?"

Randy pulled his own chair around to face hers before crossing his legs. "Hard to believe but, yeah. A cowboy, a sailor and an oil man who made the bulk of their money in panties and bras."

She toyed with her pen and studied her notes. Several seconds passed before she closed the binder. Several more ticked by before she looked up. "When you left this morning, I called you every name in the book."

Of that, he had no doubt. The only thing he'd wondered about was how long she'd wait before broaching the subject. "You had every reason."

"I thought this was a ruse." She turned the pen end over end, bouncing it on the binder. "That you brought me here because you wanted to get to know me, not because of any concern for the foundation's image."

"Actually, my concern was less about image and more about working conditions. You've seen my office."

She mulled over his admission, coming back with, "I'm an image consultant, Randy. Not a decorator."

"I know." And even knowing she wouldn't like it, he wasn't going to deny the truth. "But you're right. I brought you here because I wanted to get to know you."

She shook her head, sighed, tossed the pen to the table. "I'm surprised my making the first move didn't shoot your plans all to hell."

He laced his hands in his lap. "I committed to the consultation. Whether you and I worked out personally wasn't going to have any bearing on our doing business."

"So, what am I doing here now? Now that we've worked out." She lifted her chin; for a moment he thought it was trembling. "Is this payment for services rendered?"

He uncrossed his legs and sat forward, bracing his elbows on his knees. "This is business, Claire. Nothing more. You've seen our space, our needs. I expect you to draw up a proposal and present it. Just as you would with any client."

"But you're not just any client." She pushed up from her chair and walked to the far end of the room where, arms crossed, she stood staring out of the window.

He understood that she needed space. It just wasn't what he wanted to give her.

He got out of his seat and followed, standing at her shoulder, near enough to catch the soft scent of her perfume, far enough away not to scare her.

"You can deal directly with the partners. I'll take myself out of the equation." He'd seen her work; whether or not it was a priority, he had no doubt she could give the foundation an image befitting its purpose.

He was much more intent on what she could give him. He just hadn't yet come to terms with what that was. The scope of what she'd brought to his life.

"It's a mutually beneficial arrangement. You've gained a business contact. I now have a date for tomorrow night." He didn't say anything about sharing her bed.

She snorted. "That's hardly taking yourself out of the equation. Not to mention you're assuming I haven't changed my mind about going out with you."

"Have you?"

She gave a noncommittal shrug. "I'm not so sure I'm comfortable with the idea of being your arm candy."

At that, he moved in, settling his hand at her nape and turning her to face him. "Arm candy I can get anywhere. You're more to me than that."

She looked up, her long lashes lifting to reveal a challenge in her eyes. "What am I then? A business associate? A neighbor?"

"You're my lover." He lowered his head, nuzzled the corner of her mouth. "The only woman in my life."

She parted her lips; he slipped his tongue between before she could speak. He couldn't give her anything more. Not now. Not yet. But he could give her this. He could make certain she knew he wanted her.

The kiss went on, a gentle, teasing intimacy that

knocked him flat. She touched her tongue to his, brought up her hands to cup his face and hold him, whispering words too softly spoken for him to hear.

He didn't need to hear. He felt. The wall of his past breaking apart. The ice of his heart cracking. What he felt was more than wanting her in his bed or at his side. More than having her in his life.

She tasted like he'd come home.

"YOU HAVE NO IDEA how much I appreciate this." Claire swiveled right then left, taking in her reflection in the bedroom's full-length cheval mirror before catching Perry's reflected gaze. "The dress is perfect."

"You're welcome," Perry said from where she sat cross-legged in the center of the bed. "It's one of my favorite things, and I never get a chance to wear it seeing as how I don't get invited to many swanky Christmas gigs."

"It's not so swanky."

"Are you kidding? The Bourbon Orleans at Christmas? Think I could tag along? I can't even imagine how the place must be decked out. It's got to be absolutely gorgeous."

"No doubt," Claire said, forcing a laugh. It was Friday night, and if she could've backed out of this particular gig, she would have done so in a heartbeat.

Okay, she could have. She didn't want to.

The chance to schmooze with society's movers and shakers didn't fall into a girl's lap every day. The contacts she could make might prove to be invaluable.

Then there was the fact that she wasn't ready to write Randy out of her life. Except for those few minutes yesterday in Luther's office, all of their interaction had been one-on-one.

It was time to see if he knew how to behave in public.

She smoothed a hand over the front of Perry's velvet dress the color of gold-tipped pine needles. It was a shade of green Claire never wore, but she had to admit it worked. The spaghetti straps holding up the bodice crisscrossed through tiny loops to leave her back bare.

The only thing she wore beneath was a thong. "The back's not cut too low, is it?"

"Yes," Perry assured her. "And that's the point. Everyone will be so busy ogling your ass, they'll never notice they've been pickpocketed until it's too late."

Claire rolled her eyes, though her girlfriend wasn't totally off the mark. Festive or not, tonight's gala was still all about raising funds.

And no matter his claim that she was the only woman in his life, Randy wanted her with him for reasons that were more about business than anything. Of that, she was certain.

She had to be certain because, if she was wrong, she would never forgive herself for breaking off their fling. There was no way around it. She felt as if she'd been bought and paid for. She had to let him go.

And she had to do it now before she fell any further in love.

RANDY WAS on his way to let Claire know the limo had arrived when her front door opened. One of their neighbors—dark curly hair, gypsy look...Perry?—came out, passing him on the courtyard's walkway in front of the Christmas tree.

He nodded his head, frowned when she laughed as if keeping a secret, then returned his attention to the business at hand. At least he tried to. But when he glanced back toward Claire's place, he couldn't even remember his name.

She stood in the doorway looking like a present waiting to be unwrapped. Her hair hung past her shoulders in huge bouncy curls he itched to get his hands on. Her dress was green with a festive gold glow that did amazing things to the skin it bared—and it bared a hell of a lot.

"Wow," he said when he walked up to her. It was the only word that worked. "You look amazing."

"You don't look too shabby yourself," she teased.

He ignored the way the emotion in her voice didn't reach her eyes and made a spinning motion with one finger. He hadn't seen her since yesterday when they'd shared that kiss he would never forget. "Turn around. Remind me what I missed last night spending the night alone."

She spun, giving him a quick glimpse of her back before she faced him again. "Did you spend it at home? Or in that hospital room you call an office?"

The woman knew him all too well. "About half and half. I would've come by, but it was late when I got here, and I knew you needed sleep."

She started to reach out, stroked the pendant hanging in the hollow of her throat instead. "And you got out of breakfast in bed for a second time."

"We can remedy that in the morning." He'd reserved a room at the hotel holding the fund-raiser. He hadn't mentioned it yet. He wanted to wait, to tell her first how much she'd come to mean to him in such a short time.

He wanted to kiss her, to touch her, and was having a hell of a hard time—he was the only one it seemed—keeping his hands to himself. "The limo's waiting. Are you ready?"

She nodded, smiled. "Let me get my purse, and we can go."

She didn't invite him in while she did. She simply grabbed her purse and a lacy wrap, locked her door and headed out, never once looking back to see if he followed.

7

THE NOISE was borderline deafening. The live jazz band, the dancing and clapping, the boisterous laughter that always accompanied free-flowing champagne.

Claire had met more people than she'd ever be able to remember, and had her ass pinched too many times to count. Perry could keep her damn dress.

Randy had been so courteous that Claire was struggling to deal with the guilt that came from treating him like a casual date. She'd decided early in the evening that doing so would be the only way she'd get through the night.

When he'd come to pick her up, she'd wanted to throw her arms around his neck and kiss him senseless. Never before had looking at a man left her searching for something to say. He was built to wear Armani, the tux defining him in the same way the fedora made Indiana Jones.

Yesterday Randy had told her she was the only woman in his life, called her his lover, kissed her like he'd die without her—and done it all moments before instructing her to send him the bill for the Flatbacker consultation.

It was a great big deflating reminder of how he bought his way through life. And as much as she hated to admit it, she couldn't shake the feeling that she was here because of that very same reason. That he'd bought her for the night.

"Hello, Ms. Claire. Hope you don't mind if I borrow your corner. I've suffered fewer bruises being thrown from a bronc than I have fighting this crowd."

Claire looked over as Luther settled into the chair next to hers. "I decided sitting down was the best way to protect my, uh, assets."

Luther chuckled, a deep rumbling roar. He raised his champagne flute in a toast. "Here's to the best dress I've seen in a hell of a lot of years. If I were younger, you can bet sitting here wouldn't be about taking a load off."

A blush crept over her skin. And even before she spoke, she knew she'd had just enough to drink to loosen her tongue. "Don't tell me you're holding my age against me."

"Hell, no. It's my age that's the problem. I can't run as fast as I used to, and Randy's still a scrapper. I make a move, the boy will beat me to a pulp."

Not if you offer him cash up front, she heard herself saying. Thankfully, she was the *only* one who heard it since it was all in her head.

She handed her empty flute to a server on his way to the kitchen. "I'm thinking that by now Randy's sorry he brought me along. I haven't been the most attentive date."

"Are you kidding? He's been cow-eyed all night. He's gettin' no business done. And parties are all about business for the boy." Luther clucked his tongue. "'Bout time he got bit."

She was afraid to ask. "Bit?"

"By the lovebug," Luther said, so tickled he had a hard time swallowing the rest of his champagne.

Love? Impossible. They'd known each other since Tuesday. Yes, they'd been engaged in balcony foreplay since he'd moved in next door two months ago. But love?

She looked out into the crowd, searching for the largest gaggle of women she could find because that's how it had been all night. While she'd been getting groped, Randy had been getting, well, groped.

And because she'd been so caught up in keeping him at a nice safe emotional distance, she hadn't once thought that he, too, might be hating the attention. If nothing else, she could offer him an escape from that.

"Excuse me, Luther," she said, getting to her feet. "I'm going to brave the masses and see if I can save your nephew from the same."

As she walked away, she heard Luther laugh, a sound that had her smiling even after she hit a snag in the crowd and got hit from behind. Frowning, she glared over her shoulder and happened to catch Randy's gaze.

He stood a few yards away in the center of a bevy of beauties where the only business being conducted was the business of sex. Or so it seemed to Claire, watching one woman after another maul him.

He might not be her man forever, and her earlier decision raised the question as to whether he could be her man at all. But doubts aside, the only thing that mattered was that he was definitely her man tonight.

She headed for the circle of cleavage, stepped into the center and crooked one finger. Randy grabbed her wrist, dragged her across the ballroom, and out into a hallway used by the hotel's staff.

"What took you so long?" he asked, breathing hard and backing her into the wall.

The fire in his eyes was enough to burn her. She blew out a quick choppy breath. "Sorry. I wasn't wearing my rescue radar gear."

"You're not wearing much of anything."

She snorted. "And I have the bruises to show for it."

"I've been thinking about untying your strings all night," he said, nuzzling his face into her hair, his fingers plucking at the laces holding her dress in place.

He felt so good. He shouldn't feel this good. She hated this war fought between her body and her heart. "I thought you were here to conduct business."

"I am. I should be." He pulled back, rested his forehead on hers. "I'm having a hell of a time concentrating."

"No wonder, the company you're keeping."

He laughed, stepped into her body, pressing his full length against her. "You've got to be tired. I want to get out of here, take you some place quiet—"

"What I'd really like is to go home." He paused, then stiffened; she'd known he would. She placed a hand in the center of his chest, looked up into his eyes. "I'm not running out on you, Randy. It's just that I'm exhausted."

He nodded. "I know. It's been a crazy week."

Crazy was putting it mildly. "It's been wonderful and nerve-racking, and I'm ready to either pull out my hair or sleep for three days straight."

He grew quiet, moving away and smiling down. "If you promise to do only the latter, I'll walk you out and have the doorman call up the limo."

"I promise." She'd hurt him. She hadn't meant to. And she felt like crying, wishing for the uncomplicated days when she'd done no more than flirt with him from her balcony, wondering now if her heart would ever heal.

CLAIRE WAS READY for the new year to get here. She was tired of all the holiday cheer, tired of waiting for Christmas to arrive. And after the whirlwind of this past weekend, she was just plain tired.

Instead of going to bed after Friday night's gala, she'd packed a bag, headed to the airport and flown out early Saturday morning. She'd been in desperate need of a day or two spent bonding with her best girlfriends before she went completely insane.

Neither Alex nor Windy had been in town, but at least Claire had been able to spend time in Houston with Tess. Not that the two of them had managed to solve the Randy problem, but at least the margaritas had been good.

There was no use denying that she'd fallen for him in a very big way. The "L" word came to mind, as did a future spent at his side. She'd sworn it was too soon.

Tess had reminded her that it happened. "Love at first sight," was an adage for a reason—it set forth a general truth that had gained credit through long use.

Claire had stuck out her tongue and blown Tess a big fat raspberry. Tess, like any psychologist worth her weight, had clucked right back and flicked queso from the end of her spoon. After that, a full-fledged food fight ensued.

Thank goodness they'd been in Tess's kitchen rather than out on the town.

Now, with her cab driver paid, Claire hoisted her overnighter onto her shoulder and headed down Court du Chaud's alley toward the courtyard. The sun had set, and the Christmas trees lights blazed like an electric kaleidoscope.

Bah, humbug pretty much summed up her lack of holiday spirit. But then she turned the key in her door and was hit smack in the face with the aroma of fresh-baked cookies. Sugar. Chocolate chip. Peanut butter. Oatmeal butterscotch.

Some little elf had been busy.

Some little elf had to go.

Unless, of course, she invited him to stay, damn waffler that she was.

Heart in her throat, she tossed her purse and overnighter to the sofa and made her way to the kitchen where she careened to a stop. It wasn't an elf after all.

It was Santa...of a sort.

Randy had obviously been baking for hours. Bowls filled the sink, flour dusted the floor. There had to be twelve dozen cookies cooling and stacked on racks. But it wasn't the cookies that had her slack-jawed.

It was the clothes he was wearing.

Or rather, wasn't wearing.

She laced her hands on top of her head to keep her brain from exploding. "What in the world are you doing?"

He didn't even look up, simply glanced at the timer on her stove. "Waiting for you."

"You're baking me out of house and home." If she ate a fraction of the goodies, she'd gain ten pounds. "And you're doing it naked."

He glanced down at his apron. The tasseled end of his Santa hat flopped forward. "I'm dressed."

The apron resembled a red Santa suit, and showed the jolly man's gloved hands holding open a sack that was actually the apron's front pocket. Scribbled across the pocket—one that just happened to cover Randy's groin—were the words *Caution: Creature Stirring*.

Claire read it and rolled her eyes. "I can see everything except what you've got in your pocket. I call that naked."

"It's not naked. It's...unencumbered."

Way too much information. "Swinging free and all that?"

"No. Damn." He tugged off the hat, tossed it to the breakfast nook table. It landed on top of a cookie-filled plate. "That's not what I meant."

She came closer, reached for a just-baked cookie. Chocolate melted all over her fingers. She licked it away and asked, "Well?"

He removed a baking sheet from the oven, pulled off the hot mitts he was wearing, turned off the flame. "Here's the deal, Claire. I wanted to come to you with nothing—"

"So I see," she said flippantly, trying to hide the mix of sheer terror and joy pressing in on her chest.

He tried not to glare. "I wanted to show you I don't need what money can buy. That I don't need anything but you. I love you, Claire. It's only been days. I know that."

Oh, God. Oh, God.

He took a deep breath. "But I also know that I've been waiting for you all of my life."

"What are you saying?" she asked, though she doubted he heard her whisper.

He came closer. He was big and warm and smelled like cookies. "I'm saying that I want you. It's simple. I won't take anything less than everything you have to give."

The rest of the cookie crumbled in her hand. "I won't be a kept woman."

"That's not what I want."

Okay. Breathe, Claire. Breathe. "I won't be your arm candy."

"I don't want you to be."

He was too close. Close enough to hold her if she leaned his way. "I don't want you to think you can buy me."

"The thought never crossed my mind," he said, shaking his head.

Like she believed that. "Really?"

"Okay. Maybe once. For two seconds. Until I realized I'd rather trade in my Benz on a Camry and wear nothing but T-shirts and secondhand jeans than risk losing you."

"Oh, Randy. I love you. I really, truly do." She wrapped her arms around his neck and held him until her muscles began to ache. Even then she had a hard time letting go.

Until… "Uh, Randy?"

"Claire?"

"That caution sign on your apron?"

"Uh-huh?"

"I feel the creature stirring."

At that, he laughed.

And she fell completely and madly in love.

* * * * *

Look for Perry's breakout story in December 2006!

Pick up a copy of
Goes Down Easy *by Alison Kent,*

wherever Mills & Boon Blaze® is sold.

DELIVER ME

BY
KAREN ANDERS

1

Red Letter Nights: When desire is too hot to be kept secret...

WHEN IT CAME to seducing a man, Chloe Matthews was not fainthearted at all.

In fact, nothing about Chloe Matthews was the least bit predictable. She didn't run Café Eros in a traditional way, nor did Chloe dress to impress. She didn't wake up at a regular time, nor did she go to bed according to a timetable.

At six o'clock in the evening, she watched from Café Eros across the court as the new owner walked up to Number 10 Court du Chaud and paused at his door. Chloe felt her excitement tighten to a fine edge as he reached out and removed the red envelope tacked to the door with a little Santa pin. He winced, brought his finger to his mouth and sucked.

Of course, it would have been impossible in the dimming light and the distance for her to make out the Santa pin. She knew what kind of pin it was because she'd tacked up the envelope with her own bold hand.

Since Chloe never did the expected, it wasn't exactly a letter. It was a verse of poetry. Poetry she'd written last night after she'd seen him standing with his back against his front door, illuminated in the pool of light from the wrought-iron carriage lamp.

He'd been looking up at the sky. From her balcony at Number 9 Court du Chaud, the town house next to his, she'd seen his dark, mysterious eyes framed by thick, luxurious lashes. It had been his eyes that had captured hers. Soul deep as if he possessed all the knowledge of the ages and it sat squarely on his broad shoulders. His haunted expression begged for peace, for just a small measure of tranquility.

In that moment she lost her heart to him. His dark hair, shaggy and ink-black in the lamp's glow beckoned her fingers. Dressed in a white T-shirt, the ridges of his collarbone glistened in the Big Easy's uncommon late December heat. A barbed-wire tattoo encircled his left bicep, making him look tough. And she would have believed he was tough if it had not been for that beseeching look.

Even though Chloe thought of herself as unpredictable, one small thing about her always remained the same. As a former nurse, she knew all about wanting to help, heal, nurture. But the sadness that came with that medical profession was too much for her to bear. She'd decided that running a café would allow her to care for people and sleep at night.

She stood in her little courtyard while her waitress, Tally Addison hurried around the tables, setting up for the dinner rush. She watched as the man opened the envelope, watched as he removed the scarlet paper and unfolded it. He turned it slightly toward the light, showing his magnificent face in profile, the beautiful bone structure, the glimpse of those full lips that made a woman want to grab his chin and turn his face toward her so that she could get a full view of that luscious mouth.

Chloe held her breath as if waiting for her lover's kiss. He brought the paper to his nose and inhaled. His shoulders relaxed from the tense way he held them. She expelled trapped air on a soft sound from her throat as he closed his eyes. He ran his fingertips down over the written words and she saw his chest expand and release. Gently with his big, male hands, he folded the paper and tucked it back into the envelope. He didn't look around, but stepped into his town house and closed the door.

She turned away with a secret, satisfied smile. His reaction had sizzled through her, lightning trapped in a jar. His fingers had touched the scarlet paper as if he could absorb the words into his skin.

"Chloe, I need to speak with you."

Chloe pulled her eyes from Number 10 to focus on Madame Alain, a sweet little woman who was the court's resident busybody. She was quite French with a lovely accent and had taught French at a private girls' school until she'd retired last year. She'd lost her husband to a heart attack and Chloe suspected the loneliness prompted her to get into everyone else's business.

"Yes, Madame Alain. What can I do for you?"

"I'm having a get-together for my women's bridge club tomorrow and would love a dozen beignets."

"By what time?" Chloe asked, running through her enormous list in her head looking for a place to slot Madame Alain's bridge club goodies.

"Nine-thirty."

"I'll have them for you," Chloe promised. She would have to give up her yoga class. But that was all right. Madame Alain was a good friend and patron.

"Could you deliver them? *Merci.*" She followed Chloe's eyes and with a sly grin, she said, "He's a fine man, *oui?*"

Chloe gave herself away and blushed.

"*Oui.* I see you have noticed. I know all about him."

She left Chloe hanging and the little frisson of frustration gave way to curiosity.

"*Madame.* I have a fresh batch of chocolate almond croissants and some café au lait."

"Do you now? A tête-à-tête? How lovely."

Chloe climbed the stairs with Madame Alain trailing her. It gave her great pleasure to walk into her aromatic café. Opening up to the French Quarter, her home and business was a hop and skip from Jackson Square. The "hot" court, roughly translated in French was boxed in by French Colonial town houses gracing the gardened courtyard. At the mouth of the wrought iron gate sat Café Eros with its own little courtyard, brick walls, a gray flagstone patio and a nonworking fountain used as a circular planter, thick with daylilies, iris and aster. Close to the juncture of the café and the stairway that led to the upper café, ruby-red passion flower vines entwined lovingly around a white trellis. For the Christmas season, she'd covered the tables, set around the small courtyard with red tablecloths. The wrought iron chairs, with round seats were already covered in red, part of the allure of the hot court.

The outside and inside seating, combined together, accommodated about twenty-four people comfortably and was as cozy and friendly as a living room. She offered good food, friendly service and beignets that made grown men weep.

Painted in shades of sepia and ocher, the walls were covered with old jazz posters and hand-painted with couples in amorous embraces. On the wall behind the counter was a full-length mural of Gabriel Dampier, the pirate who had made the court famous with his bawdy exploits there.

The tables inside were small and also covered with red tablecloths. Big fans hung from the hammered tin ceiling, and a long mirror stretched down one wall. Through the day the patrons enjoyed songs from Etta James, Dizzy Gillespie and Louis Armstrong. During the Christmas season, she played lively Zydeco Christmas music. A set of French doors stood open under lace-covered windows, allowing her customers to experience the French Quarter as they dined.

For the holiday season, Chloe had strung white Christmas lights around the windows and in the back corner of the café, set a five foot Christmas tree all decorated in red from its garland to its bows and its many ornaments.

Her café was everything to her and she took loving care of it, just as she took great care in the food she prepared.

Food made people forget their worries.

Sugary beignets that melted on the tongue made customers sigh with pleasure and think of decadent Sunday mornings eating breakfast in bed with naked lovers.

Her coffee was rich, aromatic, drawing people in by the smell alone. Lonely people would strike up conversations, make friendships, make a connection.

Nothing gave Chloe more pleasure than to see the lonely become whole again.

Number 10 had that look about him.

Her curiosity piqued, she settled Madame Alain at a table close to the counter in case she had a customer come in. Setting the croissant and coffee in front of her neighbor, she said, "So?"

"His name is Jean Castille, but everyone calls him Jack. He has a sexy Cajun accent and was born and bred in Bayou Gravois," Madame Alain said in a conspiratorial whisper, even though there was no one else in the café.

"I found out from the paper boy that he got the tattoo on his arm when he'd been in the military," Chloe said in the same whisper with amusement tickling her insides.

Madame Alain nodded vigorously as she tasted her croissant. After taking a sip of her coffee, she said, "Laura Sue at the dry cleaners said he was a hostage negotiator.

He brought his NOPD uniforms there to be cleaned and pressed."

But no one could tell her what had put that look in his deep, dark eyes.

That was Chloe's mission. Well, one of her missions. The first was to seduce him into her bed where she could find out what the other half of his magnificent body looked like beneath the tight, faded jeans.

That was the reason for the red-hot envelopes.

She left Madame Alain to her treat, and stepped behind the counter, walking into the hot, steamy kitchen. She switched on the fan and stirred the gumbo she'd been simmering for an hour. Her dinner customers would be here soon, along with her night help.

Returning to the exterior of her café, she stopped dead. Jack Castille stood at the counter. He'd changed into a white T-shirt and a pair of jean cutoffs that frayed against his muscular thighs.

She looked at Madame Alain who had a rapt look on her face and a sly smile on her lips. She glanced at the bell over the door and then at him. "Sorry, I didn't hear the bell."

"No problem. I haven't been waiting long."

For a moment she savored the soft Cajun accent of his voice, a spicy rhythm that called to something restless and female inside her. She smiled at him and extended her hand. "Chloe Matthews."

With a slow, deliberate move, he stepped closer to her and slipped his big hand into hers. "Jack Castille."

Direct contact with that dark gaze unnerved her. Her, Chloe Matthews, a woman who wasn't afraid to look a gator in the face and spit in its eye. No haunted look shadowed his eyes tonight, only a blatant self-assurance that Chloe immediately liked.

This was a take-no-prisoners kind of guy and his deep,

fathomless gaze pulled at her with a mesmerizing quality she'd never, ever felt before. Gosh his eyes were absolutely, out of this world gorgeous.

"I've only lived here for a short while and I've already heard a rumor about this place."

"You have?"

"Uh-huh. Heard you make the best gumbo in Louisiana."

"She does," piped up Madame Alain.

He turned to Madame Alain and smiled, "*Bonjour,* madame. I believe it was you who told me this."

"*Bonjour,* Monsieur Castille, and you have a good memory."

"Please, call me Jack."

"I shall."

Jack turned back to Chloe and the impact of those eyes was like a physical caress.

"You ain't Cajun." He looked her up and down. "And you sure don' look like *mon père.*"

"Your father? What does he have to do with gumbo?"

"In Acadia, cooking is a man's thing. To cook your first gumbo while your friends are playing *bourree,* a Cajun card game, well—it's sort of a rite of passage."

"Maybe someday I'll have to taste *your* gumbo, Mr. Castille."

"Maybe you will." He grinned like a pirate, a wickedness that warned her he was a charming rogue. "Call me Jack."

"Only if you call me Chloe."

He leaned in, his mouth close to her ear, setting off a shower of sparks inside her. "Chloe." He said her name as if she were spun silk.

This close to him she could see the lushness of his lashes, the aching brown of his eyes, the stubble along his hard jaw.

She smiled into those eyes and he blinked. Ah, he expected her to jump back like a scared rabbit. Chloe didn't scare easily.

Reaching out, she ruffled his hair. "Have a seat. I'll get you a bowl of gumbo."

He grabbed her wrist in a sudden, lightning move. His striking brown eyes smoldering with a heady beguiling smile that made her insides turn to jelly. He raised her hand to his lips and placed a kiss on her palm. The jelly inside her went liquid, hot scalding liquid.

"I'll take a table outside."

He let go of her wrist and she stood there for a moment, her palm tingling with warmth and the memory of his soft lips.

This only made her eyes fall to his clever mouth, wondering what carnal joys awaited a woman bold enough to declare herself to him.

All in good time.

She nodded, turned and slipped through the kitchen door.

CHLOE MATTHEWS enticed him, Jack admitted, taking a sip of his coffee. But her powerful allure was more than the sum of her parts, more than her fragile, heartbreaking beauty. Or her sensual, candid eyes, the green of a seductive verdant forest. His awareness went deeper than the sculpted kissable mouth, beyond her long curly strawberry-blond hair. Chloe didn't find him intimidating. Jack chuckled to himself as he remembered how her fingers had felt against his scalp when she'd mussed his hair. Like he was a mischievous boy!

She looked like a fey creature who had just stepped out of an enchanted garden. He'd been here only a couple of weeks, but he'd seen her with her herb garden on her balcony of her town house, the air sweet with rosemary and thyme. He'd breathed deeply of the heavenly aroma of beignets, croissants and other sweet things she baked in the early morning before he went to work. He'd seen the way she'd mothered the people in this court. The wounded part of him longed to feel the soft touch of those healing hands.

He'd smelled the elusive scent of her as he'd been pressed against the counter, so close to her he could have kissed those tempting lips.

He went down the stairs and chose a table close to the heady fragrance of the red flower vine.

From this vantage point he could see right down to the end of Court du Chaud. His gaze fell to his town house door. His thumb rubbed absently against his forefinger at the pin prick from the Santa tack that had been used to secure the red envelope.

Her perfume was similar to the sweet one that had clung lovingly to the paper he'd slipped out of the envelope. The smell had gotten onto his fingertips and stayed.

That short verse written with silver ink in a beautiful calligraphy had hit him square in his libido, firing his blood and giving him a raging hard-on.

> *I like to watch you*
> *I like to watch you and think about*
> *doing wild, tempestuous things to you*
> *eager and willing to explore dark desires*
> *and forbidden fantasies.*

It had been signed simply, *Santa's Sexy Elf*. His cock twitched and tightened just thinking about dark desires and forbidden fantasies.

Chloe appeared at his table almost as if by magic. But he knew it was the carnal thoughts that had distracted him.

She set the steaming, fragrant bowl of gumbo before him. She leaned across him to set down a basket of homemade biscuits, pressing against him to snag his silverware that had been pushed to the edge of the table.

She smiled at him as she handed him the silverware. "Enjoy, Jack. You'll let me know what you think of my gumbo, and if it's not as good as your father's, lie."

He looked up at her face, her kind and gentle heart mirrored there. All he could do was think about how much he wanted to encircle her waist with his hands and drag her down on his lap. Push his throbbing erection against the tantalizing heat of her soft woman's flesh. Absorb some of that gentleness that he hungered for deep into him, a balm, a boon to his soul.

He pulled his gaze away and reached for the silverware, forcing his charming smile to hide the darkness swirling inside him. "Ah, sugar, for you, I'll lie."

"Maybe you won't have to."

"Maybe I won't."

"Enjoy your meal and when you're finished, the dessert of the day is crème brûlée. I also offer other treats and they're in the glass case near the counter."

Her husky voice slid over him making him think about what tantalizing treats she could offer him. The slick heat of her body, the taste of her skin.

Her tongue slicked over her lips and he thought about it against the hot taut skin of his body, the wet slide along the rapidly forming hard-on that hadn't quite subsided.

The rumbling of a motorcycle made Jack look away from Chloe's face. A leather-clad biker used his booted foot to set the kickstand.

The biker dismounted and looked up at Jack's town house. Jack called out and the helmeted head turned, nodded and came his way.

Chloe looked up as Jack called out. She watched the biker's progress and as soon as he got to the fountain, he pulled the helmet off. Chloe gasped and stared. It was uncanny how much he resembled Jack. This man had the same dark hair only longer and pulled off his face in a short queue at the back of his neck. He had the same tough guy look about him, but with a slightly more dangerous edge. He also looked like he needed healing. Chloe saw it in his brown eyes.

"I'll take him," Tally said as she rushed past Chloe. Chloe studied her waitress avidly as she greeted the man who could only be Jack's brother and he in turn indicated the table where Jack was sitting.

Tally handed a menu to the new customer and Chloe felt the rush of emotion so thick and heavy, she took a deep breath.

Wondering where the feeling had come from, she eyed the three people in front of her. Jack and his brother were deep in conversation and Tally was busy cleaning up a nearby table.

Shrugging her shoulders, Chloe went back up into the kitchen and prepared the crème brûlée. As soon as the top of the dessert caramelized, she picked up the bowl and returned to the lower café. Approaching Jack's table, she noticed that his shoulders were tense as he spoke to his brother.

"I don't like it any better than you do, Chris. I think you might want to bring this to the police. You know better than that—you were once a cop, too."

"Right. But now I'm a P.I. and I do things my way."

"I know, but when you're over your head, you should admit it."

"I hate to agree with you, but I think you're right."

She set the bowl in front of Jack.

She turned to Jack's brother and he smiled at her. Ah, interesting, same almost-black eyes, same mouth with the luscious lips. But if Jack was as straight an arrow as she believed him to be and played by the rules, she had a feeling this man liked to break them.

"Christien Castille."

"Chloe Matthews."

Tally came over and set a bowl of gumbo in front of him. "Chloe, my brother told me you make the best gumbo in Louisiana."

She smiled into Jack's hot black eyes and then set her gaze back onto his brother. "You tell me what you think, Christien."

He dipped in a spoon and brought the steaming, fragrant bite to his mouth. Chloe saw Tally watching him in fascination.

He took the bite and then sighed. "*Mon père*'s not going to like this."

"I would never want you boys to lie to your dad, but in this case, I think you should."

"I'm not going to be the one to tell him," Christien said, shaking his head.

"Me, either," chimed Jack.

"Enjoy your meal. It was a pleasure to meet you, Christien."

"Likewise."

Tally lingered and Chloe took her arm and drew her away. "You were supposed to leave twenty minutes ago. Don't you have a gig tonight at The Blue Note?"

"Oh no! I'm going to be late," she said, looking at her watch. "Thanks, Chloe."

Chloe followed her into the kitchen. "Christien Castille is handsome."

"Is he? I hadn't noticed."

"Tally, you haven't taken your eyes off him since he walked over here."

"His looks really have nothing to do with why I'm interested in him," Tally said.

"Why are you interested?"

"Madame Alain told me that Jack's brother is a private detective."

"So?"

She fumbled with her apron strings until Chloe settled her hands against them and untied the knot for her.

"I haven't heard from my brother in days."

"Tally, I'm so sorry."

"It could be nothing, but I'm a little worried."

"It's probably nothing. You know how he is with that crazy music scene he's into."

"I know. You're probably right. Look, I've gotta go. I'll see you tomorrow."

She ran out of the kitchen and Chloe followed. Standing at the head of the stairs, she saw how Christien followed the lovely Tally with his eyes.

Christien was finishing up the gumbo as Chloe came back to the table. They were pulling out their wallets to pay the check.

Jack waved his hand. "It's on me."

Christien nodded and stood. "I'll see you later. *Adieu*, Chloe."

"The crème brûlée was fantastic," Jack said, as Christien started up his motorcycle.

Chloe basked in his praise. "Good."

"You have yourself a nice evening."

Walking to his town house, he disappeared inside. Dusk was settling over Court du Chaud. The court would soon be awash in twinkling Christmas lights. Through many windows, Chloe could see Christmas trees, their branches adorned with homemade ornaments, priceless heirlooms, and whimsical bric-a-brac. Chloe picked up the empty bowls and took them into the kitchen.

The bell on the door sounded. Chloe stuck her head out of the kitchen. "Hi, Anna. Ready for the night shift?"

"Sure am. You're free to go."

Chloe took off her own apron, gathered the ones that had been discarded in the bin next to the door and exited the kitchen. "Call me if you need me."

"I will, but you go rest. You look tired."

Chloe smiled softly at the concern she felt radiating off Anna like a warm fire. Before Chloe left the café, she switched on her own twinkling lights to illuminate the inside windows and the outside balcony and stair rail. "Didn't sleep well last night," Chloe said as she went out of the café door, running into Claire Braden dressed as impeccably as ever.

"Hi, Chloe,"

Chloe smiled and said, "Claire. I've been meaning to ask you to join Josie Russell and me on a committee for a Mardi Gras float. Are you interested?"

Claire paused and said, "Yes, and thank you for including me."

"You're welcome. I'll call you with the details. Just leave your number with Anna at the counter."

As Claire entered the café, Chloe thought how great it was that she'd finally found her own identity. When she got to the bottom of the stairs, Randy Schneider, the gentleman that he was, waited for her to pass by before he proceeded.

"Hello," she offered.

He responded in his deep, melodious voice. "Good evening, Chloe."

Good chemistry between Randy and Claire. Lots and lots of potential, Chloe thought. She crossed the square, to the brick piazza that had been part of Court du Chaud since it was built, taking a moment to admire the beautiful Christmas tree in the center. The tradition made her feel at home, an integral part of the court. Humming "Santa Claus is Coming To Town," she made her way to her own town house.

She looked toward Jack's place and wondered if she'd see him prowling the court, those haunted eyes turned up to the sky.

2

INSIDE HER TOWN HOUSE, she dropped the aprons into her washer and started it.

She changed into a pair of short, red-denim shorts and a black tank top. Pulling her hair into a messy topknot, she entered her bathroom and filled her watering can. Out on her balcony, she watered her plants.

After taking care of her herbs, she spent the rest of the evening going over her books. Visions of dark eyes and hair kept invading, so Chloe gave up about 11:00 p.m. and went to bed.

But she tossed and turned, unable to get Jack's gaze out of her mind. Giving up, she got out of bed and walked over to her bedroom window.

She could make out his face clearly as he sat on a bench in front of his town house, shirtless, the tattoo stark against the bronze of his skin.

With the moonlight gilding his hair, he looked like a dark angel with wickedness bred in the bone.

A wickedness that called to her, tempted her. A wickedness that left her mouth dry with a hunger she'd never known before. This seductive heat spinning through her blood sang inside her veins, sang an old song and stunned her, leaving her unable to look away from his dark, haunting eyes.

She wanted to do more than heal this man. She wanted

so very much to connect with him on a level that she wasn't even sure about. One so deep, so real, so clean, it took her breath away.

She pressed her face to the glass and forced herself to breathe slowly.

She had good intentions mixed in with all this yearning.

She'd heard the road to hell was paved with good intentions. And she'd bet her dark angel knew the way.

JACK SIGHED as a cool breeze blew over his heated skin as he sat and stared up at the moon. The café was dark and silent, yet cinnamon seemed to linger in the air. He'd had that dream again. He rubbed at his face to get rid of the gruesome images. His one and only failure. He'd tried to save them, all those souls on his conscience, their blood on his hands.

He shifted and rubbed the back of his neck. Guilt, remorse, pain rose in him.

At the time, Chris had been suspended from the force for punching a defendant in court. The defendant agreed not to press charges, but insisted that Chris had to publicly apologize. Chris refused. Jack felt that Chris had just quit, disillusioned with a system that worked much too often in the criminal's favor. Jack refused to quit. He'd never quit anything in his life.

Sure he'd been required to see the shrink, but he'd mouthed all the right answers even as his gut twisted. The deaths would always weigh on his conscience. No amount of talking would change that.

His gaze shifted to Chloe's balcony, to the plants there. He'd seen her watering them earlier, her gentle hands touching the leaves as her mouth moved.

He found it so damned endearing that she talked to her plants. He wondered what she said.

He caught movement at the window, his sharp cop's eyes missed very little. So, she couldn't sleep either.

Had she tacked that envelope on his door? The scent was hers.

Hell, why didn't he just say it. He wanted it to be her.

He wanted her.

It wasn't smart. A woman like that would want more than he was willing to give. He knew it instinctively. But damn, smart wasn't part of this equation right now. Smart was about as far away as it could get.

He heard a door open and saw Chloe slip out of her town house. She glided over to him. He took a deep breath and leaned back against the bench back support.

"Hi. Couldn't sleep?" she asked, her voice hushed.

She smiled at him and there wasn't anything tentative about this woman and damned if he didn't like that. She looked so fragile and delicate with her strawberry blond hair trailing down the smooth column of her neck; tickling the hollow at the place he'd die to place his lips.

He clenched his hands and closed his eyes, burying the pain deep inside him and letting the charm flow.

"No. You?" Jack replied.

"No."

"Worries?"

She nodded, her gaze going slowly over his face as if she could read him like an open book. He shifted, caught in that magical gaze, so warm, so welcoming. He wouldn't be giving up his secrets that easily and never to this woman. His professional life in the NOPD was so removed from this courtyard with its old-world charm and its pretty flower boxes. This is what he went to work every day to shield. She was what he risked his life to protect.

A twinge of guilt, a woman falling, her dark hair spilled

over the pavement. The charming facade slipped. Her sharp gaze narrowed.

"Are you all right?"

He forced himself to relax and shrug as if it were easy. "Right as rain."

"For a minute there, you looked…like you were thinking of something awful."

"Must have been a trick of the moonlight."

Somewhere near a woman's voice, lovely in cadence and melody, began to sing.

"Who's that?" He stood and looked around.

Chloe nodded toward the center of the court. "That's Tally. She sings sometimes when she gets home from work. She's a lounge singer for The Blue Note."

"It's beautiful, soothing."

"Do you need to be soothed?"

He turned to look at her and she was standing so close he brushed against her arm.

"*Ma mère* used to sing me to sleep after thunderstorms and a bad day."

She didn't move her arm or step away from him. "What kind of bad day?"

"Fightin' mostly. I was trying to defend Christien for riling up someone else."

"The makings of a cop even then."

"How did you know I was a cop?"

"There are very few secrets here in Court du Chaud, Mr. Castille. For instance, I know that you got this tattoo in the military."

The tip of her finger brushed the barbed wire and his groin filled, hot and heavy. It happened so fast he wasn't prepared. He'd thought he was in control, but the urgency was sweeping through him in a tidal rush, hurting, hard and hammering his blood. He couldn't back away from Chloe Matthews.

He took her wrist and very slowly drew her hand toward his face. With a deliberate challenge in his eyes, he brought her palm to his mouth and kissed her soft flesh.

She gasped, so softly in the hushed night. Tally sang on about fever and wanting. He pulled her closer to him. Taking her hand he placed it around his neck. Leaning down he picked up the other one and put that one around his neck.

Very slowly he began to sway.

"The tattoo was a rite of passage. All the guys in my platoon had one."

She looked up at him and he sensed she wanted something from him, but he didn't know what. It certainly felt like it was more than he could ever give.

He wasn't a man to cut and run, but what he saw in Chloe's soft, gentle eyes made him want to bolt. He was touched by violence almost every day. It seemed wrong for him to be this close to her, afraid some of it would rub off on her. But she felt so good in his arms he wanted more.

They continued to sway, even though Tally had stopped singing. In the dark, he saw a figure run across the court.

"Chloe, is that you?"

"Yes, it's me."

"Do you have a minute?" Tally asked, apology in her voice.

Chloe pulled away, saying softly to Jack, "I've got to go."

He nodded as she left his arms and he watched her slip her arm around her waitress friend.

They went into her town house and closed the door. It was time for him to get some sleep.

"CHLOE, I KNOW it's late, but I had to tell you my brother called me just a few minutes ago and he's fine."

"I'm soooo happy. Hope you told him to call you more often so you know what's going on."

"I did. He got the message loud and clear"

"Where was he?"

"He had a gig out of town, but, of course, he didn't let me know. I'm so relieved. He promised to come over for Christmas dinner. Bree and I are going to cook."

Tally and Breanne had raised their brother themselves. Instead of going to college like they wanted him to, he'd detoured and become a roadie, getting work with whatever band was hiring. "That's great. I know you and your sister have had some tough times lately. Your brother doesn't need to add to your stress."

Tally nodded her head. "So, I couldn't help noticing that you and Jack were, um, getting to know each other."

"He's a very intriguing man."

"Is that why you tacked up that envelope to his door today?"

"Busted."

"Big-time."

"I'm getting in the Christmas spirit and leaving him little gifts. I'm Santa's Sexy Elf."

"I don't know, Chloe. He looks as much of a heartbreaker as his brother."

"Both need healing."

"I'm not into healing other people like you are, Chloe. I've got enough to worry about with my brother and my own wishes and dreams. I don't need the kind of trouble Christien could bring."

"Maybe. Jack seems much more pragmatic and Christien seems much more sensitive than he lets on."

"How do you do that?" Tally asked, perplexed.

"Do what?"

"Read people so well."

"I've got what my mother would describe as the gift."

"As in 'woo-woo' stuff like reading people's auras?"

"Not exactly, but I do get 'feelings.' Been doing it all my life, even when I was a small child."

"Be careful with that man, Chloe. I'll let you get to bed. Good night."

Chloe walked with Tally to the door. "I'm happy about your brother. See you at the café tomorrow."

But it was hard to concentrate on sleep when all she could think about was the feel of Jack Castille against her body which still tingled as if he'd left a lasting imprint. Up close he was even more striking, his skin velvety soft, his scent knee-melting.

But it was still his eyes that got to her, those dark orbs to the soul. He'd been hard-pressed to disguise his pain from her. The charming smile hid a secret she was going to ferret out of him. She was obsessed by it. If a wound wasn't drained, it would fester until its poison killed.

And Jack Castille had too much of a dazzling soul for any of that blinding beauty to be dimmed.

IN THE MORNING, Chloe rose groggily and immediately headed for the shower. The memory of the feel of Jack against her last night fueled her imagination. Instead of her hands sliding over her body, they were his hands, his mouth kissing her neck, making her body tingle with a heightened awareness that she'd never felt before. She shivered under the hot spray, her hands cupping her breasts, sliding between her legs, finding the hard, hot bud of her clit. She cried out softly, closing her eyes against the pleasure that snapped through her body at the thought of Jack's fingers touching her.

She leaned back against the heated tiles and stroked her aching flesh, kneaded her breasts until she exploded in a strong, stunning orgasm.

After she dried off and got dressed, she went to her

Queen Anne writing desk and pulled out a piece of scarlet paper along with a red envelope.

She wrote the verse that ended up taking two pieces of her spicy paper. Before she went down to open the café for breakfast, she grabbed another Santa pin and tacked the envelope to his door.

Whistling a soft tune, she opened the door to her café, and stepped inside. As she walked into the kitchen, she heard the bell. Chloe set down the freshly washed aprons she'd brought from her town house and turned as Tally came into the kitchen.

"Need help with the beignets?"

"Sure, but you didn't have to be here for another two hours."

"I know, but I couldn't sleep with all the strange noises in my house. I thought I'd give you a hand."

"You do know that your town house is supposed to be haunted?"

"Of course I did. My uncle Guidry told me all about the legacy of the town house and the haunting of Dampier. When Bree and I inherited it, we had to do a lot of renovations to the place to make it into two separate living areas, but it was worth it. We both wanted to live in a haunted house."

"Is that so?"

"Sure, maybe I'll find the treasure and solve all my problems."

Chloe laughed. "You're not afraid of Gabriel Dampier's ghost?"

"No, and if I see him, I'll make him tell me where he buried all his treasure."

They laughed together as Chloe measured out the flour for the day's beignets. But as she worked silently with Tally, her thoughts drifted to Dampier. Pirate, thief, swordsman, businessman or savior, Dampier's legend was well known in Court du Chaud. Complex in nature, shrouded in mystery, and a larger-than-life personality, he lived on in the role of auspicious hero even two centuries later.

It was the title of hero that earned him his entrance into the city and his place at Court du Chaud. For their heroism in the Battle of New Orleans during the War of 1812, General Andrew Jackson fulfilled his promise to see that Jean Lafitte and his brigands, including Gabriel Dampier, were exonerated of all criminal charges, releasing Dampier to live as a free man. But when society turned their backs on him, he thumbed his nose and built the "hot" court. Now mystery and legend surrounded the court and the residents whispered of treasure and voodoo curses. Chloe always speculated as to why she'd get this terrible wash of pain through her every time she passed Tally's town house. Perhaps Dampier's ghost did haunt Court du Chaud. She wondered why and what would put him to rest.

The day turned out to be very hectic, and at two o'clock in the afternoon, the radio announcer broke into a lively Waylon Thibodeaux song with a newsflash. There was a robbery in progress at the MLS Bank and Trust downtown and shots had been fired. The announcer went on to report that the police had surrounded the bank trapping the robbers inside.

Chloe stopped stirring the jambalaya she was cooking for dinner, her heart in her throat. She felt edgy and scared, but she had a sense that not all her feelings were her own. It happened in a split second, and she couldn't be totally sure.

As the afternoon wore on, and in between serving customers and cooking, Chloe caught snatches of newscasts as reporters broke into the lively Cajun music with other bulletins. It seemed the bank robbers had taken hostages and had barricaded themselves inside the bank. At the moment it was a standoff. The announcer reported that a hostage negotiator had been called in.

She wondered about Jack and the on-again, off-again feelings of jagged fear and gut-tightening pressure that had plagued her all day.

By the end of the day, Chloe, exhausted, left the café and immediately noticed that her red envelope was still tacked up on his door. Uneasy with the turn of events, Chloe went into her town house and tried to keep herself busy. Giving up at nine o'clock, she turned on the news to find there had been no progress in the hostage-taking.

When she went to bed, the situation was still the same. She thought about Jack and the stress he must be under every day at work. It didn't surprise her that he looked so haunted. She said a silent prayer for him and drifted off to sleep.

In the morning, before Chloe went to work, she checked the news and discovered that the hostage situation had lasted through the night and now was in its second day.

While working, Chloe listened to the radio, but nothing changed, nor had it changed by the time she walked up to her town house that night, and she went to bed worrying about Jack again.

JACK MASSAGED his lower back as he walked past Café Eros, the smell of crawfish stew hung in the air along with the yeasty smell of rolls. His stomach rumbled with hunger. A balmy breeze tousled his hair and the billowing curtains from Chloe's bedroom windows looked ghostly in the moonlight. His back was stiff from the hours he'd stood outside the bank trying to talk to panicked robbers bent on escape. He'd kept them busy while, only hours ago, S.W.A.T. had successfully taken them down without losing one hostage. Adrenaline from the rescue still pumped through his veins. Jack knew how easily things could go wrong when negotiating with desperate people.

From several yards away, he saw the red envelope hanging on his door with another Santa tack. Suddenly his weariness disappeared and he reached out for the envelope. He brought the paper to his nose and breathed deep. This time there was no mistaking the heady perfume. It was Chloe's.

He opened the envelope and pulled out the folded pieces of paper and read.

Watercolor Fantasy

I thought about you today in the shower where I had a watercolor fantasy. It was uncontrollable while my soapy hands slid up and down my skin.

I thought about your smooth palms, fingers splayed against my skin, the beauty of your large, warm hands moving over the places where I caressed—my thighs, my stomach, my breasts.

I thought about your powerful body against mine, your male energy mingling with my female energy, a tangible force that vibrates with crystal sound.

I thought about your warm chest pressed to my back, about your clever, wet mouth on the back of my neck. With a soft sigh, my back arched helplessly in anticipation of such an exquisite sensation.

The heat of the fantasy made me melt. With eyes closed to savor the pleasure, I said your name longingly and the melody flowed and combined with the mist.

Like an echo, your name returned to me glittering like stardust against my wet, heated skin.

I wrapped my arms around the diamond bright drops to hold you against me, to drink you in to assuage a powerful thirst.

I thought about your face, eyes closed in pleasure, dark lashes brushing strong cheekbones, a sculpted mouth created for smiling, for pleasure, for a woman's lips. My lips, I thought, just mine.

I thought about encircling your wrists to savor the soft skin there. Ride with them on the journey over my body that feels like a part of yours. It's as if we were connected by a thread that draws us irresistibly toward each other with unrestrained and explosive force.

The hungry promise of your mouth on mine entices me to turn into your arms. The heavy fire in my aching nipples can only be quenched by contact with you, such sweet, intense satisfaction.

The pressure points of our bodies touch, my softness to your hard, heat. Your name falls from my lips again an aching whisper. Jack.

Wherever you are your head lifts and you smile with a secret knowledge of your own watercolor fantasy that I thought about you today in the shower.

Santa's Sexy Elf

Jack stood there for a moment looking at the erotic words. A fire of need gripped his body, and he automatically turned to look at her town house. Of course the windows were dark and no one stirred. It was 3:00 a.m. and Jack hadn't eaten in over twenty-four hours. He'd been in the same clothes that long as well. He reached down to his doorknob and disappeared inside his place. He stripped down to nothing, his fully aroused flesh throbbing. He walked into his bathroom and turned on the shower.

Stepping beneath the warm spray, he grabbed up soap and quickly washed himself. He sent the soft, fluffy towel over his highly sensitized skin, unable to stop the flow of charged electricity that sizzled through his body. The woman knew how to write a poem. The erotic words set off another charge of electricity. Jack had to stop for a moment and get his breathing under control. He went into his bedroom and pulled on a pair of gray shorts.

His body hummed with anticipation and he ignored that voice in the back of his head that told him he was acting like a hormone crazy fool. Chloe Matthews was in her town house fast asleep from a long day at the café, he was sure. But he couldn't wait until morning to see her. He couldn't wait another minute.

3

WITH A HARD, hollow ball of longing lodged in his chest, he rubbed at his breastbone. The loneliness had intensified and it was Jack's own fault. He'd distanced himself from human interaction. It'd been a slow, painful process.

Pushing those thoughts from his mind, he turned his attention to Chloe and all the little puzzle pieces he had yet to find to complete his picture of her.

It took him moments to get to her door. He raised his hand and knocked.

After a few moments, the door opened and she stood there, her hair a wild mass around her head, her soft gaze alert and unsurprised.

That hollow place inside him ached with a rawness that slammed him hard. She was so feminine and graceful, and the heat in his body jumped like an inferno.

She wasn't his type. Not at all. He usually went for curvy, carefree girls with uncomplicated brains, women who wanted nothing more from him than a good tussle between the sheets. He didn't know what Chloe wanted and yet he felt something about her drawing on him, and him alone. Instinct told him his curiosity could be dangerous, but the warning wasn't strong enough to overpower the attraction.

All thoughts flew out of his head when she reached out and cupped the back of his neck, her small hand soft and warm. With a husky voice filled with rich promise, she asked, "Have you been thinking about me, Jack?"

CHLOE TOOK a quick intake of breath at the scorched feel of Jack's skin, the wet strands of his hair cool against her hot flesh. Dark stubble lined his jaw, and his almost black eyes were vivid and captivating against all that sinful, unruly hair.

She'd endured days of feeling ardent and restless with a delectable, overwhelming kind of need. The sight of him kindled a flame inside her, making her hunger for the pressure and tang of his lips against hers, and his slow, long-fingered hands caressing her naked flesh, awakening her body with his touch until the ache inside her was an all-consuming burn.

He was drawing her through a portal into another dimension where sensations were sharp; the emotions thick and electric, they left her skin tingling. Jack, an unruly man with a burning look, took her on a wild ride every time she met those haunting eyes. The man who hid his pain behind the facade of a charmer.

But Chloe wasn't fooled by that wicked, melting grin. She wasn't fooled by his casual stance, the overly confident persona he projected to protect himself.

Drawing him into her town house, she closed the door and found herself pressed up against the wall with six feet, two hundred muscle-packed pounds of aroused male surrounding her.

She wanted to do so much more than heal him. Her body responded to his as she responded instinctively to that intense awareness sizzling between them.

She knew what he needed now was human contact, physical release. Chloe reached up, sending her hands over the rounded bulge of his biceps to the tense muscles of his shoulders. "Easy, baby," she soothed.

He breathed a violent breath. "Not just yet, easy is for later. Right now I need hard and fast."

Her heart swelled at the vulnerability in his voice. It was low and shaky, ragged with desperate longing.

"Take off my shorts, Chloe. Touch me."

Her hands went to his hips and she pulled at the soft cotton waistband. He was naked beneath and she cupped his hot, hard erection in her hands, stroking him.

He cried out, thrusting his hips toward her. His hand slipped to the straps of her nightgown as he pushed one then the other eagerly from her shoulders. The silky material skimmed down her body in a shimmering, liquid slide, caressing her heated skin. She pressed her breasts into his hard muscular chest.

Her hands grew bolder and Jack's eyes darkened. Reaching down he parted her legs, sliding a finger inside her slick, wet sheath. She arched again. This time he captured one of her taut nipples, sucking her hard. Her hips pulsed eagerly as he slid his slick finger in and out of her.

He lifted her against the wall, wedging his thighs between hers, the heat of his body like a brand against her flushed and aching skin.

Chloe arched into his touch, helpless to do anything but gasp for breath. She was aware of the wall, cool and solid against her back, but her focus was on Jack, on the hunger that was threatening to devour them both.

He pushed himself against her wet, ravenous sex with teasing thrusts that made her pant with frustration.

"Jack, please," she begged.

Chloe cried out as he entered her fully in one driving thrust. She wrapped her arms around his neck, welcoming the deep, smooth strokes of his body inside hers.

He withdrew, and thrust again with a groan of pleasure. His words, low and wild, said in Cajun French.

"Yes, Jack. More, harder."

He lost his control completely, she could feel the change in him, in his hard body as he pressed against her, delivered more power with each thrust, and she was trapped in the savage heart of a hurricane. He called out roughly as he drove into her. His slamming thrusts made her cry out in sheer carnal satisfaction. Every part of her welcomed him, the harsh sound of his breath in her ears, the breathtaking, sliding friction.

Dragged into that maelstrom like a rag doll, she gave herself up to the sensations. She wanted to soothe and entice him, to break down his walls and let loose all that dark pain. She stared into his face, fierce with passion. With his sweet voice in her ear, he exploded, sparking off her own hard, dazzling orgasm.

For a moment she caught a glimpse of his eyes, saturated with pleasure so deep she could hold it for only a moment. He buried his face into the hollow of her throat, his chest rising and falling against her heated skin. Gently she tried to raise his head, wanted to see that look again, wanted to absorb the intimacy, but he refused to raise it.

She clasped her arms around his neck and knowing that the feelings were not all hers, dissolved into tears. These tears were not of pain or sorrow, but were sympathetic, swelling currents that purified and enhanced her. Tightening her hold, she let the feelings wash through her, she didn't try to stop them, didn't hesitate. The feeling frightened her. It was dangerous to want a man so much, dangerous to think that she alone could bring his secrets into the light of day.

Jack looked up, his eyes hypnotic as she stared into the dark orbs. He reached and very gently wiped at a tear with his thumb.

"It was so intense. That's all," she said.

He released her, her slick body sliding down his muscular frame. "A woman's tears don't frighten me, Chloe." He tenderly whisked away the moisture from her other cheek. "I want to discover all the ways you express the energy I see in your eyes."

"Come."

She took his hand and led him to her bedroom. There he let her pull him down onto the mattress.

He curled around her, dragging her as close to him as she could get. He sighed softly as if he was exactly where he wanted to be, was meant to be. The vulnerability spoke to her. She soothed her hands down his back, touching her mouth to his shoulder with little kisses. Trailing her mouth up his neck, she buried her nose into his still damp hair, breathing in the exquisite scent of him.

They slept then and sometime before dawn she was awakened to the feel of his tongue stroking along her collarbone. Then his mouth was on her breast, and desire sluiced through her.

She allowed herself to lie back and enjoy the delicious sensations Jack aroused. They rendered her incapable of doing anything more than experiencing—the rasp of his tongue against her nipple, the tug of his lips as he sucked at her, the play of his fingers over her rib cage.

He took her nipple tenderly in his mouth and nipped at it gently with his teeth, and she cried out at the searing, bright heat, just slightly painful, but oh-so-arousing. She clutched his head against her chest, shaking with pleasure as he pressed her breasts together and took both nipples into his mouth.

She was so sensitized to his touch that when he slipped his hand between her thighs, she had to breathe deeply to absorb all that she was feeling, bringing her so close to climax. She moaned deeply as he slid his long finger inside her. He murmured softly in appreciation, and slid in a second one opening her, making her wet with need.

His clever hand caressed her sensitive folds and furrows with tender skill, petting and coaxing her tirelessly until she crested and came.

Time elongated and night, a blanket of shimmering pleasure and feverish need turned toward dawn. She didn't know how many times he brought her to orgasm. It all seemed to move together in one timeless, shivering current. He was insatiable, ravenous; taking her tender flesh as if he fed on her very desire. He pushed her further than she had ever dreamed of going, until she was writhing and pleading, her hands tangled in his hair.

Snaring the back of her knees until her widened thighs were draped over his, her pelvis was now tilted up, yielding to him. He eased over her, using his thighs to push hers up higher on his waist. With his exquisite body, he trapped her beneath the satisfying weight of all that muscle. His forearms came to rest along either side of her face and he shifted his hips, fixing the thick-sheathed head of his penis firmly against her very essence.

Looking intently into her eyes, he entered her slowly, letting her feel the size of him, teasing her with the promise of more.

He thrust into her, strong and deep, entering her to the hilt with the first unrestrained push. She gasped on a stunned breath as her inner muscles contracted around his shaft.

His eyes widened in response, revealing heat, and something else battling in their depths. Before she could analyze that last emotion, before she could dwell on the initial pleasure of being thoroughly consumed by him, he began to move, his body undulating and grinding against hers as he increased his rhythmic pace.

A low throaty, ragged moan escaped him, and he took her mouth, kissing her with an out-of-control, potent passion that caught her off guard. His tongue swept into her mouth, matching the rapid, hard driving force of his hips and the slick, penetrating slide of his flesh in hers.

Tremors radiated through her from the sensitive spot where they were joined so intimately. She felt thoroughly possessed by him, body and soul.

She concentrated on what he was giving her, how alive he made her body feel. Running her hands down the slope of his spine, she slid her fingers to his buttocks, grasping the hard pumping muscles and locked her legs around his waist to pull him closer, and surrendered to her body's keening demand for release.

This time he was right there with her when she reached the peak of her climax. Groaning, he broke their kiss and tossed his head back, his hips driving hard, his body tightening, straining against hers.

"Chloe." Her name growled out between his clenched teeth as his body convulsed one final time.

He lay on her for a few minutes and they rolled to the side. When Chloe caught her breath, she turned toward him. His untamed hair was dark against the white of her pillow, his handsome face in shadow. She turned to her side and propped herself on her elbow.

Gently, she pushed his damp hair off his forehead and he opened his eyes. Quick as lightning he captured her hand and brought it to his mouth. His soft lips caressed her fingers, her palm and wrist, sending heat into her veins. She met his eyes, getting lost in their depths.

With his other hand, he captured the back of her neck and brought her mouth down to his.

"Do you want me to go?"

Chloe smiled, feeling so deep in her bones that he didn't

want to go, could feel the quick rapid beat of his heart as he waited for her answer.

"No. Do you want to go?"

He brought her down against his hard, muscled chest. "No. I don't, Sexy Elf."

"How did you know it was me?" She absently caressed his chest with her hand.

"Your perfume." He kissed the top of her head. "I have a confession to make."

"What would that be?"

"I wanted it to be you."

"I was worried when you didn't come home," she whispered.

He shrugged. "I worked the hostage situation."

His breathing increased. She instantly felt nervous again. "So everyone is okay?"

"Yes."

She turned over and placed her forearms on his chest and leaned into them, gazed up at him, a question on her tongue.

"Sleep now. I'll make you breakfast in the morning," he said effectively curtailing anything else she wanted to ask.

Chloe sighed. Pushing him wasn't going to make him open up. She could feel his resistance.

She snuggled down against him and closed her eyes, but she was very aware it was a while before Jack slept.

4

JACK WOKE in Chloe's arms. She had herself wrapped around him, her sweet face pressed against his back. He gently shifted until he could look at her. She continued to sleep. He continued to watch her and thought he'd never seen a woman more at peace than Chloe.

Her life here in the court was idyllic. He came from a much more chaotic part of New Orleans. One that required he be a street fighter just to survive. Taken in by the illusion they could make the world a better place to live, he and his brother had joined the NOPD. Christien had been a damn fine cop, but that boy hadn't been able to handle the rules and regulations the law required. He'd chafed at the system, claiming it worked against the police more than it helped them.

Jack knew the system was flawed, still, it was the system they had. And he was loathe to leave it.

Christien seemed to have settled down as a P.I., but Jack wasn't convinced that his brother was happy now that he was no longer a cop. Jack guessed that Christien couldn't let go his former profession. Using a lot of contacts in the police department to get the information he needed to do his job effectively kept him connected.

Chloe shifted and a lock of her red curly hair fell across her beautiful face. He reached over and took it between his fingers, rubbing the softness.

She opened her green eyes and smiled so sweetly, he leaned over and kissed her mouth.

"Good morning, handsome," she said, her eyes still sleepy.

"Are you one of those cheerful morning people?" he said with mock disgust.

"'Fraid so, mister. I pop out of bed with a smile on my face and whistle a merry tune while I'm talking to the birds and little woodland creatures."

He chuckled. "Is it contagious?"

"It could be. If you hang around more often, you too could be talking to the birds yourself."

"Sounds like a good plan to me." He smiled.

His cell phone rang and he reached across her to fumble for it in the pocket of his shorts.

"Hello," he said, his voice raspy. "Chris. What's up?"

He settled back against the fluffy pillows.

Chloe slipped out of bed completely naked and stretched. Enjoying the view, he slowly slid his gaze upward. His mouth went dry as he took in curvaceous hips, a slim waist, and breasts, perfectly rounded, tipped with succulent pale pink nipples. She bent over and picked up a flowered robe off the floor. Shrugging into it, she looked over her shoulder at him and smiled like an angel—a direct contradiction to her blatantly seductive pose. Jack lost his mind.

"Jack? Jack!"

"Sorry, I got distracted. What did you say?" he said slipping easily into Cajun French.

"Jolie's been trying to call you. You know how little sisters can be. I figured you were working that bank hostage scene. You okay?"

"Feeling great."

"Call her, she's worried."

"I will."

"You're going over to *père*'s on Christmas Eve, right?"

"Plan on it. I'm bringing someone with me," he said. He hadn't expected that to come out of his mouth, but he wanted her to meet his father. He was sure that Gerard Castille would like Chloe Matthews very much.

"You are? Would she have vibrant red hair and the prettiest green eyes this side of the delta?" The woman in question came out of the bathroom. She twisted her strawberry blond hair into a topknot with an enameled chopstick, smiled at him again and kissed his forehead as she walked past the bed, her soft, captivating scent lingered after she passed.

"She would," he replied, feeling an almost caveman-like need to physically protect the jewel he'd found. "Don't tell me you're interested because you are too late brother."

"*Non.* I have my eye on that pretty little waitress."

"She looks like a handful."

"I sure hope so. You should have Chloe bring her gumbo and *père* can decide if it's better than his." His brother covered the phone and Jack could hear muffled conversation. "Listen, I've got to go."

"Are you working?"

"Yeah, so I'll see you on Christmas Eve."

"I'll be there. Be safe."

Jack lay in Chloe's bed and took stock of her bedroom. The bedding was covered in a sumptuous lime-green quilt made of smooth, delicate silk with a soft cotton blanket, and comfortable sheets beneath. The wrought-iron bed frame supporting his back had a matching footboard with intertwined flowers, pure New Orleans. On the bedside table were many different crystals, a blue beaded voodoo doll and white candles burned down to almost nothing. The scent of lavender pervaded the room. His Chloe was a metaphysical woman. It would be another layer of tempting personality to discover.

"Hey," she said from the doorway. "Are you going to join me in the kitchen? I love to talk as I cook."

He swung out of bed, watching as her green eyes ignited from within when she took in his naked form. "You are beautiful."

He smiled and looked at her, then gestured toward the table. "Fear evil voodoo spirits?"

"Don't scoff. I think Captain Dampier walks the court at night."

"Dampier? He's dead."

"Not all things pass into the afterlife."

"Chloe, ghosts don't exist."

"This one does and he's under a powerful spell."

"*Gris-gris?* Like in a curse? If he's under the spell, then he's probably harmless."

"When I sense him, he's not alone. The feeling I get from this other is…malevolent. So, I take precautions."

"You sense things like a psychic?"

"I can see right away that you're a skeptic, but you can't deny there's energy in what we did last night. In the very air we breathe right now. Why not believe that the spirit exists after our mortal bodies succumb to death?"

He clasped her around the waist and settled her into his lap. "I can't deny that energy, Chloe. But voodoo curses?"

"I can't believe that you've lived in the bayou and don't believe in curses. What kind of self-respecting Cajun are you?"

"I believe people think there are such things, but I live in the real world that's curse enough."

Her eyes softened and she cupped his jaw. "Do you want to talk about that?"

He felt all the pain, loneliness and doubts crowd at the

back of his throat. The scent of this woman, her magical green eyes and silky hair made him long to release all the pressure of holding all those emotions at bay. He closed his eyes to get himself under control. He couldn't bring that evil into her bedroom. He shook his head. "Nothing but ugliness there."

He turned his head and saw the painting above her bed. It was a watercolor in a circular pattern, the background bisecting the painting with turquoise above and midnight blue below. Vibrant color mixed and blended to form a feast for the eyes.

"What's that painting?"

Chloe looked up at it. "I haven't had time to paint since I opened the café. Too busy. Same with the potpourri in the corner there on my desk. I used to mix it and sell it at the café, but now I don't have time."

"You did this painting?"

"Yes."

"Is there a story behind it?"

"You're changing the subject, aren't you? It's the chakras."

"A what?"

"Chakras means wheel in Sanskrit and corresponds to seven essential psycho-physical aspects of man."

"What does that mean exactly?"

"Places on the body. The third chakra is located in the solar-plexus." She touched his chest, outlining his pectoral muscles as if the tip of her finger was dangerous to his skin. "It corresponds to the element of fire, the color yellow and holds important aspects of willpower, self-confidence, forming relationships, social identification and the drive for power and achievement."

"How can you tell if this particular chakra is not working right?"

"Lack of self-confidence, low self-esteem, inner discontent and restlessness and the suppression of emotions."

Jack didn't want to go down that slippery slope. "Is there one for sex?"

Chloe smiled and laughed softly, the ripeness of it like a berry on his lips, the tantalizing juices sweet and tart all at once. He wanted to hear that sound again. "You *would* be interested in that."

"Well, is there?"

"Yes, there is. Both females and males have a root chakra where all energy is focused, for you, it's chakra one."

He raised his brows. "You bet it's number one."

She smiled quickly. Her hand trailed down his body to his abdomen and he sucked in a breath at the heat of her touch. "Here," she said, stroking his stomach, brushing over his genitals. "And here."

Slipping her hand to his lower back, she breathed, "And here. For me, it's chakra two and is associated with water and the color red."

Heat blossomed in his groin and his cock hardened.

"No problems there," she said softly. "Have you ever tried Tantric sex?"

"No."

"Want to?"

"There's only one answer to a question like that."

She laughed again, the sound like tinkling chimes. She moved off his lap and settled into the middle of the bed. Patting the space in front of her, she said, "Sit here and cross your legs."

"You're not going to make me chant."

She laughed again and realized he was addicted to the sound.

"No, silly." She removed her robe.

When he reached out to her, she said, "No, no touching

yet." She sat in a cross-legged position and said, "This is called soul-gazing. It's said a woman can orgasm from this alone. Jack, look at me. The eyes are the windows to the soul and can transmit a lot of sexual energy."

"Chloe, I'm not sure I'm the right type of person for this."

"You don't have to be, Jack. Just open yourself up to new possibilities. Look into my eyes and let me look into yours."

"Into my soul?"

"Yes, if you'll let me."

Since he was sure this was going to be some kind of sexual game, he smiled roguishly and nodded. "Eye contact and the big O-mmmmmm. I'm ready."

She looked at him trying to suppress a laugh. "Get serious."

His eyes locked with hers and the humor quickly left him. For a moment he stared at her, then he seemed to sink, as if he were going under into the deep depths of an emerald pool.

Power surged around him, the energy flowing from her and back again. His energy met hers and blended like vibrant colors mixed on a rich red canvas, achingly beautiful to watch. His body tingled and throbbed, pleasure running like notes on his skin, playing a song of desire. "Chloe," he breathed softly.

"Look into my eyes, Jack. Just look."

He welcomed the rush of adrenaline spiking through his veins, his heart pumping hard in his chest in thrilling anticipation of the fantasy unfolding before him.

His excitement sped, warring with his need to touch her. But true to his promise he kept his hands and body immobile.

He looked deep and discovered that she was a generous person, one who overextended herself. One with a beautiful soul.

Chloe's eyelids drooped, her breathing increased as a

moan escaped her lips. Instead of that jade sea, he was now immersed in a volcanic fury, with purple flames licking at him. The power let go of him with a heave.

Chloe's eyes widened, her pupils dilated until there was almost no green left, the black swallowing him whole. She arched her back, her nipples forming into stiff nubs. Her whole body pulsed so hard, Jack felt the vibrations all through his legs, groin and abdomen.

He closed his eyes because he didn't want to come. It shocked him how close he was to the edge.

"Damn," he muttered, reaching for her. When his hands slid over her thigh, Chloe cried out, flowing toward him like water. The thick moist air made it all but impossible to breathe. A tropical storm, water pounding, heat rising. Fire and water mixing to make…steam.

He pulled her beneath him and couldn't stop. He touched her hair, his fingers combing through, tangling in the luxurious strands, a mass of orange flame.

With the colors of the rainbow dancing in his eyes, he lowered his mouth to hers, thrusting into her at the same time, unable to stop the greed in his body from overcoming his need to pleasure her.

But even in his greed he gave, his pulsing shaft going deep into her wet heat.

A groan ripped out of him as his body shuddered. The feel of her hands on his back was like a sensual goad that made his hips move faster, his skin sensitized beyond belief.

"Chloe." He said her name on a groan. "It's too much." Fears unbidden leaped through him like blinding light. Sending him careening.

"No. It's all right," she breathed into his ear. "It's all right."

Her eyes locked on to his, open, dark with passion, filled with a steadiness that grounded him. Beneath the passion, he saw a trust that humbled him.

Rocked to the core, he held her close. His heart thundering against hers, his body taut as a wire. Fears melted away. There was no room for them when his body was vibrating from dozens of more vivid sensations. When he took her to the peak again, he rode out the storm, glorying in it, desperate for more.

He held back, gaining his pleasure from hers, stunned by the way she responded to each touch, to each kiss. Her beauty was his, her sincere and generous heart as well. With the breath laboring in his lungs, the blood pounding in his head, his body screaming for release, he thrust into her with a motion bred from a dark need inside him, reaching for the purity of the light he saw in her. Vanquishing the pain that pulsed in rhythm to his surging blood, an ache that festered in his soul. Knowing that this woman could heal him if he let her throbbed through him.

Deeper, he slipped deeper, filling her, rocking her toward that final crest. When she cried out, her body shuddering, he buried his face in her hair and let himself follow.

THE SMELL of breakfast woke Jack, and he followed his nose to her kitchen.

Wrapping his arms around Chloe's waist, he said against her ear. "I promised to make you breakfast."

"It would give me a whole lot more pleasure to cook for you." She turned in his arms and smiled up at him and he felt as he never had before.

"Don't you get sick of cooking? Working seven days a week in that café has to tire you out."

"No, in fact, I opened a café so that I could cook all the time."

"When do you do things for yourself? You mentioned painting and your potpourri mixing. These are things you enjoy, right?"

She shrugged. "Along with yoga. But when you own your own business it dictates the hours."

"Sure, but you could hire help to give you a hand."

"I'm used to working a lot. I had a big family and my father died when I was nine. I helped my mother with four siblings, including a set of twins, so a horde of starving people is right up my alley."

"Nine years old?"

"No choice. After my father died, my mother had to work and I needed to pitch in."

"How old are your brothers and sisters?"

"My sisters Lacy and Savannah were seven and five and my twin brothers Cade and Cameron were three."

"Where are they now?"

"Lacy teaches archeology at LSU, very studious. She loves to dig in the dirt for old bones and such. Savannah plans wild bachelorette parties, enough said there. Cade owns a crawfish business, so I get my crawfish wholesale. Cameron just got out of the Marines. He works for the government and travels a lot."

"Sounds like they all did fine."

"They did and I'm very proud of them."

"So I guess you all have a big Christmas get-together."

"Sure, a big meal on Christmas Day."

"Would you like to see how Cajuns celebrate Christmas?"

"Are you inviting me?"

"Sure. My family isn't as big as yours. You've met my brother, Christien and I have a sister, Jolie. She's a lawyer, but don't hold that against her."

"I'll tell you what. I'll go to yours if you come to mine."

"That's a deal, Ms. Matthews. Now, can I help you with breakfast?"

"No. Sit down and tell me about your two tense days."

"Nothing to tell. We beat the bad guys."

She turned from the stove and frowned. "I'm curious about your job."

"I go in when there's a crisis situation and hostages are involved. Otherwise, it's routine, like standing a post."

"I'm not asking for the specifics about *what* you do, but how you do it."

"What do you mean?"

"You showed up at my door obviously needing… comfort."

"I wanted you."

She sat down next to him. "Do you think that sex isn't comfort? It's a release of tension, sure. We do have sexual tension, but it's more complicated than that."

"Chloe, I have a shrink at work. I don't need one at home."

"Do you talk to your shrink?"

"I don't really need to. I handle what I need to handle when I need to handle it."

Those deep green eyes were aglow. He gazed into them realizing she could see all the way through to his soul and knew every nuance of every cell there. He wondered if she was getting one of her "feelings" right now. It didn't matter. He wasn't talking about his job.

None of that ugliness belonged here in Court du Chaud. He did what was required of him.

She smiled a soft wistful smile and returned to the stove. For some inexplicable reason, he felt bereft as if she'd imploded and all her beauty and caring had left with her. What was with this woman that he wanted to spill his guts to her? Make that sparkle shine in her eyes and make her look at him with the tenderness and care he'd seen there last night when she opened the door. He'd moved so close to her in just a handful of hours. It was unsettling.

He pushed his chair back and approached her. "Chloe, look, I'm sorry, but it's not something I want to talk about."

She nodded her head, but didn't face him, he couldn't stand it. He clasped her shoulder and turned her. "I don't talk about it because it makes it too real. Especially here in this court. It's like a Christmas postcard with the big tree in the center, your café filled with light, the place alive with activity."

Her expression was serious. "People live their lives here, Jack. It's not a fantasy. What you do for a living is real, too, and you can't hide from reality. I know, Jack."

"I like my illusions, Chloe. Peace is really hard to find and I moved here to get some of it. It's the most idyllic place I've ever seen."

The corners of her mouth turned up, but her smile was dim. "Who am I to disturb the peace then? It's time to eat."

They dug into their eggs and Jack felt like a kid who wouldn't share his toys. But his toys were violent and dangerous and he didn't want Chloe exposed to that kind of hostility.

She, more than anyone, was such a part of this court. Her café sat open and welcoming, just like its owner. And she reigned over the court like a queen. Everyone loved her. He could understand why.

"So does Madame Alain know all that goes on here?"

Chloe smiled, the twinkle back in her eyes. "She's lived in the court the longest of any of the residents. What she doesn't know she'll ferret out. She loves discovering all the court's secrets, so don't expect this to stay quiet too long."

"As soon as she sees the smile on my face, she's going to know what we've been doing."

Chloe laughed. "You're right. I wish everyone could have the same experience."

"To hell with everyone else. This experience belongs to you and me," he said, giving her a special grin and rising from the table.

"Wait!" Chloe popped a piece of toast in her mouth, getting up from the table with the plate of half-finished eggs in her hands. "I'm not done yet."

He stalked her around the table as she scooped up a fingerful of eggs and slipped them into her mouth. Jack watched rapt as her pink digits disappeared between her lips. "Doesn't matter, this goes beyond food."

Sliding her fingers slowly out of her mouth, she asked coyly, "Are you saying sex is everything?" She set her plate in the sink as he came for her.

"Are you saying it's not?" He pressed her against the nearest wall and braced his hands on either side of her head, his hips pushed deeply into hers. She gasped. So perfectly fitted to her, he likewise gasped when she pushed back.

"Bite my tongue," she invited, her voice husky and enthralling.

"If you insist." His lips covered hers, his tongue invading the warm recess of her mouth sucking on her tongue and gently biting. "Damn," he murmured against her mouth, then along down her chin, which she tilted up, offering the tender skin of her throat. "I can't believe how much I want you again."

He unwrapped her like a Christmas present, reverently, knowing the gift beneath was everything he could ever want. When his hands delved between the folds of her robe and touched creamy skin, he was lost, then found as her arms came around him.

5

"Let's lay here for the rest of the day," Jack suggested.

"That would be nice, but I've got to get to the café. There's baking and the lunch and dinner menus to prepare. Chloe ran her hand up his chest to his jaw, his skin moist and smooth beneath her palm. "I'm sorry." Resentment worked its way from a small bud into full bloom. It twisted inside her like barbed wire. She also had responsibilities and people who depended on her. Torn between her need to serve the people of the court and wanting to get closer to Jack, to discover what he was trying to hide, made that resentment easy to taste. But her café was a popular spot and people expected her to be there. Yet, Jack wouldn't open up to her. Wouldn't talk to her about what was bothering him. Even a simple discussion about yesterday made him pull tight into himself. Still, her sense of him grew stronger each moment she spent with him. That darkness inside him was eating him alive, and he didn't realize the danger he was in.

"Too bad. I have all day free. Come on, play hooky."

"No, Jack, I really can't. I have a large order to prepare for a customer, deliveries and all the rest."

"So is your café doing pretty well?"

"Yes, I'm solid."

"Then why don't you hire more help?"

"I have Tally and Anne."

"You work seven days a week. Why not take Sundays off?"

"I can't. Running a business is time-consuming."

He scowled and made no move to get up.

"Come by the café for lunch and I'll fix your favorite dish," she cajoled. "What is it?"

"Chicken, shrimp and andouille jambalaya."

"Yummy. I can make that for you with some crusty French bread, a nice crisp salad, some wine."

"Sounds like you have enough to do today. Why don't you make me something special some other time?"

"No. I can do it. No problem. Walk me down to the café?"

After going to Jack's town house so he could get dressed, they crossed the court, passing the large Christmas tree and piazza. Chloe went to ascend the stairs when a pair of well-worn boots caught her eye. She walked around a group of bushes to find a boy nestled in the branches.

"What are you doing in there?"

"Nothing."

She took in his tattered clothing and the look of hunger in his eyes. Fear, desperation beat at her senses. "What's your name," she asked gently.

"Vincent St. Claire."

"Hi there, Vincent. How old are you?"

"Almost seventeen."

"You looking for work?"

The boy straightened and stared at her, hope fresh and clean pulsed across his face.

"Yes. I could work for food."

"Nonsense. Three squares are part of the deal and minimum wage. That okay with you?"

"Yes," he blurted.

She felt the shock of his good fortune long before she saw it in his eyes.

"You can start by getting over to Foster's two blocks over, and getting yourself a pair of black pants and two white dress shirts. Here's an advance on your wages."

He looked down at the money she'd pressed into his hands. Then up at her as if she were a Christmas angel just appeared to him.

"When you get back, there's a broom in the kitchen. I'd like you to sweep everything inside and out. Then I'll teach you how to set up the tables for breakfast. I'll need you to bus tables when the crowd starts getting thick. Think you can do that?"

"Yes."

"What are you waiting for?"

When the boy ran off down the street, she turned toward the café.

"I hope you know he's not coming back."

"He will. Oh, don't go all NOPD blue on me, Jack."

"How can you be sure?"

"I'm sure."

"Whatever he does, that was generous of you, but you have to be careful, Chloe."

"You told me to get some help. I got help."

"You know what I meant."

"Stop fussing and I'll get you a beignet that'll make you weep into your café au lait."

Chloe was true to her word and Jack enjoyed the pastry as the boy came back with his purchases. She told him to wash up and change in the bathroom. When he came out, she put him to work.

The day was grueling and Chloe kept on, long into the night. She smiled as she made a note to herself to make some sexy sugar cookies for her friend Josie Russell for Christmas Eve, two days away. She couldn't believe Christmas was almost upon them. Josie had lived at Court du Chaud her whole life and befriended Chloe when she'd opened up Café Eros and moved into the square.

She actually should say she was baking *more* sugar cookies, since she'd baked several dozen for her friend since Thanksgiving. She hoped Josie knew what she was doing with number seventeen's current occupant, the globe-trotting, high-powered shark, Max LeClerc. Max's grandmother had passed away, so he was back to take care of the sweet woman's belongings. Chloe's chest got tight when she thought of Nana LeClerc and her penchant for thick chicory coffee. If Max hurt Josie, she'd make sure his next batch of cookies had appropriate messages on them like *get lost* and *you suck*. Even with the Mardi Gras committee, she and Josie hadn't seen each other recently. They were long overdue for a girls' night out.

WHEN SHE WAS ready to close up, she came out of the kitchen. Vincent was sitting at one of the tables studying the mural of Captain Dampier.

"Vincent, you're still here?"

"You didn't tell me I could leave."

"Sure you can. Thanks for your help." She felt his immediate fear as he looked out the dark windows. "Vincent. Do you have someplace to stay tonight?"

"I could go to the shelter."

"I've got a small room in the back. It's not much, but it's clean and there's a bed. I use it sometimes when I get a break. There are some books in there, a lamp and a small TV. You'll have to use the restroom to wash up, but it's available if you want it."

"*Do I?* Thanks, Ms. Matthews."

"Call me Chloe. I forgot to ask you. Did you deliver Madame Alain's lunch to her all right?"

"Yes and she speaks French."

"She does. You were gone a long time."

"She pulled me in the house and talked my ear off. Asked me a lot of questions."

Chloe smiled. "Did you endure it okay?"

"I did. She wants me to come back again to talk. She's a nice lady."

"Did you get enough to eat?"

"Yeah. I mean yes."

But she saw the way he eyed her case. "You know, I forgot to wrap up these beignets and they'll be stale by the morning anyway. Why don't you take them back with you?"

"Thanks, Chloe."

He clutched at the small sack he'd been carrying when she'd met him. "Do you have everything you need?"

"The shelter gave me the necessities."

"Good. I'll see you in the morning. Good night, Vincent."

"Good night, Chloe."

When she slipped past him, she felt a warning, a tremor of something dangerous. She looked at the painting of Dampier. "Are you up to your old tricks?" she murmured under her breath. But she felt nothing else.

"Good night, Captain," Chloe whispered as she went out the door and locked it.

CHRISTMAS EVE day Chloe had given Josie her box of wrapped cookies, still chuckling about the spicy messages she'd written on each one. Josie was going to kill her.

She closed early to get ready to meet Jack. She'd missed him the last two days. He'd been called into work, but he promised her he would be home in time for them to go to see his parents and siblings in Bayou Gravois.

The days still hadn't gotten cold, so she kept to her lighter clothes, a red stretchy top that clung to her rib cage and a short flirty skirt with holly leaves and berries decorating the slinky fabric.

Just as she was putting the finishing touches on her makeup, there was a knock on her door. She opened it and greeted Jack with a kiss that was soon hotter than both of them could help. His hands did quick work with destroying her carefully coiffed hair.

"Hey, Chloe. Time to *laissez le bon temps rouler.*"

"Let the good times roll. Agreed."

"You made gumbo?"

"I thought I'd give *ton père* a run for his money."

"He loves a challenge." Grinning, he leaned and caught her chin in his right hand, stroking the pad of his thumb across the lush swell of her lower lip. "You look good, *mon couer.*"

My heart. That's what he'd called her. Chloe jerked back from him, batting his hand away. Her hold on her emotions and her libido was tenuous at best when this man was around.

"Ah, what you do, sweetheart." He brushed his thumb over her lip again.

"Stop. I don't want to be late and you've already made a jumble of my hair. Now, you can spoon the gumbo into the bowl while I go fix your mess."

She laughed as he kissed her neck and wiggled out of his grasp as he grinned at her.

"Go. Fix. I'll do as I'm told. *Mon père* will have my head if I'm late."

Later, as they passed the café, Jack asked, "How's that kid working out? He giving you any trouble?"

"No. He's a hard worker. I let him stay in my back room."

"In the café, when you're not there? That's not a very good idea, Chloe. Maybe you should cut him loose."

Once they reached the car and got settled inside, Chloe

explained, "I think if Madame Alain has her way, she'll adopt the boy. She's teaching him French whether he wants to learn or not. The whole court has embraced him. He's doing odd jobs for a lot of folks."

"Does he have a place to be tonight?"

"Ah. There is a heart buried in all that cop cynicism."

"Does he?" Jack repeated. "If not, we'll bring him with us. One more won't be a problem."

"You're too late. Madame Alain has asked Vincent to celebrate Christmas Eve with her, but you are very sweet to offer."

"Sweet, yeah right."

"So what can I expect tonight? I hope there will be dancing."

"You won't be able to avoid it. My family opens up the parlor, moves the furniture, everyone's required to dance."

As they drove along the Mississippi, Jack said, "There's a legend that says Cajuns used to set elaborate fires along the river. Beacons to guide *Père Noel*'s visits by pirogue. And to light the way for the faithful to attend Midnight Mass."

"What's a pirogue?"

"A Cajun canoe."

Soon they were turning into a driveway in front of a beautiful house. Once inside, Chloe was inundated with hugs from people she didn't know, but laughed and joined into the rolicking good time. Loud music was playing, a large Christmas tree sat in the foyer, the rest of the house adorned splendidly for the holiday season with fresh fruits, winter berries, garlands and magnolia leaves, and full of magnificent period antiques.

"Your parents' house is magnificent."

"Where you at, T-Jack?"

Jack turned at the sound of the woman's voice. She was

gorgeous. Dark hair, dark eyes, exquisite bone structure. Chloe was immediately jealous.

"Ah my Le Le. Where you at, little sister?"

Chloe relaxed her taut shoulders.

"Jolie Castille." The woman held out her hand. "You must be Chloe. Jack told me all about you."

"I hope not everything." His sister's curiosity assaulted Chloe's senses.

"Only that you believe in a *gris-gris* ghost." Jolie shuddered. "Scares me."

"Ghost? What ghost?" Christien asked as he slapped his brother on the back and spoke to him in French.

"Gabriel Dampier." Chloe was once again caught by the striking resemblance the brothers had to each other. Their devil-may-care attitude washed across her senses.

"That old legend. Chloe, you should be ashamed of yourself," Christien admonished.

"Why you keeping this flower at the door?"

A tall, lean man with graying hair and a twinkle in his eyes was the spitting image of his sons. "What you got in your hands?" He leaned forward. "Gumbo." He looked at his son. "You make this to show up *ton père,* T-Jack?"

Jack smiled and said, "*Non, mon père,* Chloe made it."

"It's good, pa," Christien said.

"True? Better than mine?"

"You've got to taste it," Jack said, glancing at Chloe and giving her a wink.

Jack's father led Chloe to the living room. Turning down the music, he announced to the whole room what she suspected was that she was trying to upstage him. The whole room burst into laughter. Jack's father then took her by the arm to the kitchen where a big black pot was cooking over the stove. The smell was heavenly.

He took the plastic bowl out of her hands and threw the contents into a pan and turned up the heat. When it was hot, he collected two spoons. Meanwhile, the family had pushed their way into the kitchen as Jack's father brought the gumbo to his lips. Chloe was proud of using the Cajun dark roux, a concoction of flour and butter cooked for twenty minutes to a thick consistency and added to dishes, namely gumbo. It took skill to obtain a dark roux and Chloe had perfected it over the years.

Jack's father tasted his own and then tasted hers. His eyes got very round and he turned to look at her. He took another taste. *"Il est meilleur que le mien. Le secret est dans les roux!"*

Everyone laughed. Chloe looked at Jack. "What did he say?"

"It's better than mine and…"

His father slapped her on the back. "The secret is in the roux," Jack's father translated.

The room was so full of joy and good will, Chloe's senses went crazy. A full grin split her face. She took the spoon out of his hand and dipped it into the pot. Taking a taste, she rolled her eyes in pleasure. "It's wonderful."

Jack's father gave her a quick nod and yelled out, "It's time to eat, then we dance!"

Jack bent down and whispered in her ear. "Looks like you're an honorary Cajun. No one's ever bested my father at gumbo."

Exhausted from dancing, her stomach full of food and beer, Chloe settled down for the traditional opening of the gifts. She proudly presented Jack's father with her gaily wrapped package and encouraged him to open it. When he did, he slapped his knee, laughing so hard his face turned red. He held up her homemade roux for everyone to see.

***

IT WAS CLOSE to one o'clock when they got back to Chloe's town house. Once inside, Chloe went into her bedroom and came back with a small, wrapped package.

"Merry Christmas, Jack."

He pulled the wrappings off. Inside was a small rectangular yellow and golden brown striped stone on a black cord—a tiger's eye.

"It's a very powerful protective stone. It also balances emotions and aids in clear insight. I figured as a police officer and hostage negotiator, it was a perfect choice."

His heart leaped in his chest. This woman who he'd only met days ago had become so important to him. The fact that she accepted what he did without protest, without trying to change him was a precious gift. It made the protective instincts rise like a living thing inside him. Everything he could do to protect her innocence and genuine spirit he would do.

"Thank you."

"Tell me…why did you became a police officer?"

She took the cord out of the box, her hands warm and tingly on the back of his neck as she set the clasp. She arranged the stone against his skin and he grabbed her hand in his, pressed it against the hollow of his throat.

"When I was six, a man broke into our house to rob it. My father was hurt and my mother was killed."

He heard her take a ragged breath, saw how the information made her eyes tear up. His soft-hearted Chloe.

"Oh, Jack…" Drawing a tremulous breath, she slid her arms around his waist. "I'm so sorry," she whispered, her face wet against his neck, her voice breaking.

Tucking her head tighter against him, he savored the silky disorder of her hair. "It was a long time ago, but I wanted to do something to keep people safe. I know I can't protect the world, but at least I can do my part."

"You don't have to tell me any more, Jack. I can feel it. It burns in you like a pure flame, so much an integral part of you."

He felt her catch an uneven breath, and he tightened his hold, experiencing a sudden thickness in his chest. How had he gotten so lucky to find a woman who thoroughly understood him?

She pulled her face away from his neck, her eyes shining with tears. "Now where's my gift, Castille?"

He laughed, hugging her against him. "On your balcony."

"Oh yeah?"

He clasped her hand and led her up the stairs to the top floor of her town house, through the fragrance of her bedroom.

He pushed the doors open to reveal the earthy smell of her plants, the wooden bench settled among the greenery, a scarlet throw a splash of red against the warm wood, a mini oasis inside a bustling city. His gift stood in the center of the balcony with a good view of the court and all the way to the Mississippi. An easel with a white canvas positioned on top with brand-new paints set on a small mosaic table, and a small wooden stool.

She turned toward him, a fairy princess bathed in white moonlight, her hair pulsing with fire, her green eyes alight with passion and pleasure.

Maybe it was the magic of Christmas, maybe it was his wayward heart, but he was in free-fall, knowing without a doubt that this woman was his. He didn't know where the feeling came from, but he knew that she belonged with him, his match.

He loved her.

The knowledge swirled inside him with a powerful, blinding force that made him reach out to her, remove everything they wore with an efficiency that left him breathless. Her breasts were like alabaster, tipped with cotton candy-pink, beckoning him to taste, her eyes a luminous lush green filled with healing refuge, and caring.

He sank into her eyes like pools, immersed himself until he felt as if he was drowning.

SHE WAS DROWNING in the deep dark wells of his eyes, opaque in the moonlight as if light were absorbed instead of reflected, broadcasting his wicked intent. He was tall and leanly muscled, his black hair stark against his tan skin. The magic of the night swelled around them, the energy their bodies created crackling and spitting tangible power. Sexual power, the power of love.

She loved him.

A warm wind cascaded over them, exerting gentle pressure on her body, propelling her into his arms. She pressed him back to the bench, arranged the throw around him and made him sit.

"Chloe," he said, his voice hushed and fierce.

"In time, Jack, in time."

She wanted to paint him with all that energy and power radiating into the night. In the most magical night of the year where love pulsated in the heavens and people everywhere celebrated wondrous events.

She let herself go like she hadn't in a long time, realizing that work had consumed her, dimmed her by slow degrees until she was a shadow of her former vital self, but with Jack's gift, she was beginning to think maybe she was spreading herself too thin.

As she looked at him, the colors formed in her mind and she put them down on the canvas, painting in almost a trancelike state.

His need seemed to pulse in the night, his heartbeat loud, the desire fiery and thick with passion. Clean, blue shot through with silver, showing protection and honesty. The darkness that was inside him, a dark sickly green that made her want to walk over there and soothe him, but the painting consumed her until she was spent.

Without a word she walked over to the bench and climbed onto his lap, her mouth connecting hot and wet with his. She pressed her aching breasts to his mouth and cried out when he bucked up against her, embedding himself to the hilt. She inhaled sharply at the abrupt invasion, and he groaned, long and low. He rocked her pelvis against his, his body tense and quivering. She grabbed on to his shoulders, easily picked up the rhythm he set, and rode him with utter abandon.

He circled his tongue around one rigid nipple, blew a hot stream of breath across the peak, then did the same to the other. He lapped at her slowly, licked the taut tips teasingly, and nibbled until the madness was too much to bear. Grabbing a handful of hair from the back of his head, she pressed his parted lips to one aching, tingling crest in silent demand, and he obeyed, taking as much of her breast as he could inside the wet warmth of his mouth.

He sucked, and she felt the tugging, pulling sensation all the way down to her sex. She couldn't stop the whimper of need that started deep inside where Jack filled her, full and throbbing. She moved on him, harder, faster, and came undone as an exquisite torrent sent her careening into an intense orgasm.

He released a harsh groan of surrender then and gripped her hips, rocking her in time to each frantic upward surge of his thick shaft within her. She wrapped her arms around him, holding him close as his own body shuddered in and around hers in long, deep, powerful spasms.

When it was over, they melted into each other, their arms and legs entwined. Both of them too wiped out to move. Chest to chest, the wild beating of their hearts was all Chloe could feel, and in that seemingly endless stretch of time, that profound connection between them was all that mattered to her.

6

JACK'S CELL PHONE rang and Chloe moved off him, wrapping the scarlet throw around her shoulders. Following him into her bedroom, he picked up his jeans and extracted the cell phone.

"Castille," Jack said into the receiver. After a few moments, he nodded. "I'll be right there." He turned to her as he started to dress. "I'm sorry, Chloe. I've got to go. I'll call you when I can."

He kissed her soundly on the mouth and then was gone. Chloe walked back to the canvas, the colors bright in the moonlight. She saw Jack racing across the court to his car and heard the engine turn over—disturbing the still quiet of the night. The moonlight dimmed and when she looked up a cloud had obscured the silvery light.

Something dangerous whispered on the air and Chloe shivered.

HER EYES popped open and she knew. She knew something terrible had happened. She looked at the bedside clock, seeing that she'd only been asleep for two hours. Throwing the blankets away from her body, she immediately felt the cool air. The moon was totally obscured now and the temperature had dropped significantly. She dressed quickly in the darkness. She had to get to the hospital. That's all that pounded in her brain. She had to get there.

Utter chaos reigned as Chloe burst through the emergency room doors. Her eyes scrutinized the many faces. She passed two police officers arguing with a man in handcuffs. Firefighters were everywhere. Chloe searched for Jack and finally found him sitting on a gurney in the main hallway. His eyes were closed and his head rested against the wall. She saw that his shirtsleeve was bloody and her heart climbed into her throat.

"Jack!" she called as she came up to him.

His eyes opened and he looked at her as if for a moment he couldn't place her.

"How did you know I was here?"

"I just knew. I think I knew when it happened. I needed to make sure you were okay. What happened?"

"Some guy washed out of the firefighter trainee program and decided if he took firefighters hostage they would have to reconsider. Started a fire in a building and when they showed up, he grabbed them."

"The guy who's in handcuffs?"

"Right. I went in to talk him down. One of the firefighters panicked and I pushed him out of the way. Bullet caught me in the arm."

"So why is he at the hospital?"

"I wrestled him to the ground and got the gun away from him. He got a little bruised and battered in the struggle. Cut his eye and they thought he had a broken arm. He's waiting to be X-rayed." He sat up and then winced, grabbing at his arm. "What are you doing here?"

"Don't move. I'll get someone to give you something for the pain."

His grip was firm as he latched onto her wrist. "No. Chloe, go home."

"I'm not going home when you need me."

His eyes desperate, he said, "I don't need you. The doctor is busy with other more serious cases, burns and smoke inhalation."

"I'm not leaving, Jack."

He tightened his grip. "This is not the kind of environment for you, Chloe. Now listen to me. Go home."

The man in handcuffs passed them, keeping up a nasty stream of profanity. Jack closed his eyes as if he could shut out the scene and make it stop by not looking. But reality was just as ugly as the man's words, as ugly as the kernel of doubt building in Chloe. "I'm going to get someone…."

"No, dammit, Chloe. Leave, now. You can't do anything for me but get in the way."

Tears stung the back of her eyes at his harsh tone. His dark eyes were glassy and unfocused. He sat here all alone with no one to tend to him and he wanted her to leave. How could she when her feelings went far beyond care? She was in love with Jack, in too deep. "Why won't you let me care, Jack?"

"I appreciate that you care, but I can't have you here. Go back to Court du Chaud. You don't need to see this."

"That's what you're afraid of? I'll be exposed to this. I'm stronger than I look and I'm not the kind of person to turn away from someone in need."

"That's right, Chloe. You are the court's little helper. When do you take time for yourself? When do you say enough is enough?"

"What is that supposed to mean?"

"You give to everyone. When are you going to see that it does nothing but string you out?"

"Is that how you get through each day? Turn yourself off from your emotions?"

"We're not talking about me."

"No, let's talk about you. Let's talk about how you shut me out of this part of your life. You shut off your emotions and they're eating you alive."

"Drop the subject, Chloe. You don't want to know about that dark side."

"Yes, I do. Don't you get it? I love you. I want to know everything there is to know. It's all or nothing, Jack."

"Then it's nothing," he said looking away.

She stood there for a minute letting those words sink in. "You can't mean that? After all we shared. You can't mean that."

"I can't talk about it with you or anybody. Go back to the court where this kind of thing can't touch you."

As Chloe ran out of the hospital, Jack felt as if he would collapse into himself. He just couldn't do it. If he told her, it would come rolling out of him in a wave of ugliness. He would protect her instead and make her understand when he got home. He would make her see that it was best that she not be part of *this* world.

CHLOE REFUSED to shed a tear all the way home. At her town house, she decided she'd work on something that would distract her thoughts—like her potpourri. When she heard the knock on her door, she found Jack standing there.

"Chloe, I need to talk to you."

She brushed past him and went out into the court, thinking she'd get in her car and drive, when movement in her café caught her eye. There should have been no one there. She changed directions, walked up the stairs and unlocked the café door.

Pushing it open, she came face-to-face with Vincent. He was standing over her broken lock box, pointing a gun at her with his right hand and holding a wad of cash in his left. Her cash.

"Chloe, you're going to listen to what I have—"

Jack never finished what he was saying as he took in the

situation. She felt him move and when she looked behind her, she saw that he'd pulled his gun.

"Vincent, put the gun down," Jack ordered.

"No," Chloe said, her heart pounding. The kid was stealing from her, after all that she had done for him. Chloe came face-to-face with her own fears. Who was she kidding? She couldn't nurture everyone. She couldn't make all the hurts go away. He was in her café. The place where she spent most of her time. And now, as she was looking down the barrel of a gun, she realized that she hadn't lived for herself. Not truly lived. Not for herself. "Vincent, take it. Take it all and leave. If this is what you want, go ahead."

"Chloe!"

"No, Jack," she said touching his forearm and making him lower his gun. Turning to Vincent, who grimaced as if he was going to be sick, she said again, "Go. Take it. It's not worth it. Not worth dying over."

"I'm sorry," Vincent said, his voice breaking. "But I thought you were going to throw me out."

"Why would you think that, Vincent?"

"Him. I heard what *he* said last night. I *heard*. I'm sick of going hungry. I appreciate what you did for me Chloe, but I was scared of being on the street again."

She moved away from Jack. "Vincent. I wasn't going to throw you out. Jack is a police officer and naturally suspicious of strangers. He was just trying to look out for me. Please, put the gun down and everything will be okay. We won't speak of this again."

"Chloe, no," Jack said from behind her.

She turned to him. "It's okay."

She moved closer to reach out her hand. In the moment, the only emotion she could feel reverberating around the room was fear.

She walked up to Vincent. His eyes went from her to Jack and then, miraculously, he put the gun in her hand.

"I'm sorry, Chloe."

JACK STOOD THERE while Chloe spoke quietly to Vincent. He'd confiscated the gun and found out it wasn't even real. His arm throbbed in time to his heart, the adrenaline of the past six hours suddenly making him exhausted.

Chloe came over to the table where Jack was sitting. "That was armed robbery, Chloe. It's a felony."

"It wasn't even a real gun, Jack."

"It doesn't matter. We perceived it to be real."

"What if I don't press charges?"

"Since robbery is a crime against a person, there's not much I could do if you don't."

"Jack, he was scared. I just want to forget all about the incident."

He nodded. "I agree with you and part of it was my fault. I'm sorry I scared the kid. It doesn't seem like Vincent will give you any further problem."

"Thank you for letting me handle it."

"You were right. I haven't given you enough credit."

"I helped my mother raise four children, Jack. I know what hardship and pain is all about. I might not be catching criminals every day, but that doesn't mean it can't encroach on Court du Chaud. We just have to deal with it."

He was quiet for a moment before he finally asked, "Do you still plan on going to see your family for Christmas?"

"That's right. It's Christmas day. They're expecting me at noon for Christmas dinner."

"Do you still want me to come with you?"

She looked away. "That depends, Jack."

"On what?"

"On you."

He stared at her for a second, knowing how foolish he felt, especially after this incident. "I'm sorry for what I said in the hospital. I realize now I can't protect you from everything and everyone. It's hard to admit to myself. That's what I've been harboring. I tried to save a woman and her family once and I failed. Their deaths were a hard thing for me to accept. Still are. I feel I made a mistake somehow and caused it."

"You can only do what you can do. I realize that now, too. When Vincent had that gun on me, I thought I haven't done nearly everything I wanted to do. I've given up a lot for my café and the people of Court du Chaud, but you're right. I need help. This business has grown beyond me. I need to take time for myself."

He took her hands in his. "I love you, Chloe. We'll take all the time we need for that."

"Yes, we will."

AND THEY TOOK the time they needed that afternoon—to drink wassail, eat Christmas ham and all the fixings at her sister's apartment surrounded by all the people who meant so much to Chloe.

Later that night, as they walked across the court back to Chloe's town house, Chloe smiled when Jack stopped walking and gave her a slow smile.

"There's another red envelope on my door."

"Looks like it."

"Do you think it's from my Santa's Sexy Elf?"

"I wouldn't jump to conclusions until you have all the facts."

He enfolded her hand into his and brought her with him to his door. He pried off the Santa tack.

He took a whiff of the scarlet paper. "Smells like the same helper."

Jack pulled the paper out of the envelope and read the words silently, but Chloe knew the poem by heart.

Elemental Love

*Earth: Emerald shades of stability
renewing itself
once touched by love
we too become solid as earth.*

*Water: Sapphire shades of flexibility
there is power in softness
victory is yielding
Water like love seeks all openings.*

*Fire: Scarlet shades of hunger
altering lust from empty frenzied need
to a glowing, hot heart of golden passion
Fire tempers the combustion of emotion into love.*

*Air: Silvery shades of enigma
Air and love share the secret of invisibility,
whispered on the air of our emotion
the heart divines the secret.*

Chloe

Eyes warm and full of the love he had for her, Jack leaned in close. "Could you paint this on a canvas for me?"

"I've already painted it. I'll show you."

He squeezed her hand before she could go any farther. "Merry Christmas, Chloe."

"A very Merry Christmas, Jack."

He took her in his arms and pulled her tight to him and they stood for a few moments in the balmy air. He tugged her toward his town house. "Show me, later. Come, *cher,* share my bed."

Chloe, filled with so much happiness, took his hand this time as they went into Jack's house and closed the door.

THE DAY AFTER Christmas, Chloe left the warmth of Jack's arms to open up her café. But when she arrived, everyone from Court du Chaud was already there and somehow they had learned of the events of the previous day. Madame Alain, no doubt. Tally was behind the counter, the beignets already baked. Josie Russell took Chloe by the arm and made her sit down. Then Jack walked in with a smug look on his face. "It was you," Chloe accused.

"Yes. I told everyone what a treasure they could have lost yesterday."

He sat down at the table while Tally served them.

"Beignets and coffee for everyone, Tally. On the house," Chloe said. She leaned close to Jack as she took a bite of the flaky pastry and gave Tally a wink. "The girl is learning," Chloe said, taking a sip of her café au lait. "I think I'll get a chance to get to an early morning yoga class more often."

Chloe took his face in her hands, feeling such a rush of love for him that it made it hard to breathe. "I love you, Jack Castille and your whole family," she whispered brokenly. "God, how I love you."

Stroking her hair gently, he gazed at her, a heart-stopping smile in his eyes; then he lowered his head and kissed her in front of everyone. Her neighbors, her friends—her family—roared and clapped. Jack looked around. "That's what it's all about, *cher*," he whispered back, his mouth moist and warm against hers. "That's what it's all about."

* * * * *

Karen Anders cooks up a special treat with Tally and Christien's steamy story in Give Me Fever.

Available at your favourite retail outlet in November 2006.

SIGNED, SEALED, SEDUCED

BY
JEANIE LONDON

1

Ma chérie,

You outdid yourself with your sexy performance last night. I still can't get you out of my head. The way you stripped off that dress, exposed your beautiful body inch by glorious inch. You took such care peeling away your hose, your hands sliding over your legs, tempting me with each slow stroke. You seduced me as you explored your desire. And watching you touch your most intimate places turned me on....

Je t'ai regardée. Je t'ai désirer. Maintenant je veux te toucher.

La veille de Noël
Number 16
Court du Chaud

JOSIE RUSSELL REREAD the message inside the Christmas card, had been rereading it since awakening this morning to find it inside her foyer. The bright red envelope had her name scrawled in bold letters across the front, an adult version of handwriting familiar from long ago. The card inside was simple and tasteful, the sort a man might choose.

A man had—the man who also happened to be her one-time neighbor across the alley and the full-grown version of the boy she'd had a huge crush on while growing up.

He'd slipped the card through her mail slot during the night, sometime after she'd closed the curtains on another nightly striptease in front of her open bedroom window.

Last night hadn't been Josie's first performance.

For weeks now, she'd been involved in a sexy seduction that had prompted her oh so handsome audience to leave cards and gifts on her doorstep.

One morning, he'd sent a compilation of sultry tunes and a belly chain of hand-wrought gold links and tiny diamonds with a request for her to dance. Another, he'd sent a designer set of sensual oils along with an antique Tiffany lamp and a request for her to pleasure herself in the soft light.

He'd refused to play the spectator any longer, and as Josie skimmed her gaze over the familiar bold scrawl, she savored a zip of forbidden pleasure at the words.

Je t'ai regardée. Je t'ai désirer. Maintenant je veux te toucher.

I've watched you. I've desired you. Now I want to touch you.

At least she thought that's what the card read. No doubt he also remembered how horrible she'd been at French. He might have left his family home in Court du Chaud over ten years ago and not looked back, but he wouldn't have forgotten her struggle to learn the language when she'd been nothing more than his best friend's pesky kid sister.

Maybe he thought she'd finally mastered the language. After all, she was New Orleans born and bred, and ten years was a long time. She'd grown up during those years.

So had Max LeClerc. The boy she'd moon-pied over for

so many years had grown up to be entirely scrumptious with his tawny blond hair and deep blue eyes.

Glancing at his signature, she let the full impact of the words filter through her, a pleasure she refused to feel guilty about. Not after fantasizing about Max since she'd been old enough to understand what a fantasy was.

La veille de Noël.

Christmas Eve.

Max would unwittingly indulge her fantasy by giving in to the attraction that had flared unexpectedly between them since his return home. He wanted to take their unusual flirtation across the alley for one night—Christmas Eve.

I've watched you. I've desired you. Now I want to touch you.

Josie wanted him to touch her, too.

The timing couldn't be more perfect, either.

She'd always adored Christmas, but ever since a mysterious gift-giver had rescued her from a lonely holiday vacation when she'd been sixteen, Josie had had a thing for secret Santas.

She'd never discovered who her champion had been all those years ago, but she thought it fate that Max would start sending cards and gifts now, a not-so-secret Santa of sorts, which could only mean they were destined to play out this fantasy. And time was running out. He'd told a neighbor he would be leaving the court right after Christmas.

Tomorrow was Christmas Eve.

With that thought, Josie decided to forego coffee. Bypassing the kitchen, she went into the hall to grab her coat and purse. She tucked Max's Christmas invitation into a pocket, picked up her briefcase and locked up the house, set on a course of action.

Max's request had changed everything, and she had preparations to make to honor his request in style.

Stepping out into the unseasonably warm December morning, Josie smiled at the well-known sight that greeted her.

Court du Chaud.

French Colonial row houses surrounded the courtyard tucked cozily away from New Orleans' busy French Quarter. Only a few blocks from Jackson Square, the "hot" court, as it roughly translated, connected to the busy city by a wrought iron gate and an alley.

Every resident of Court du Chaud knew the story of this historic courtyard's notorious origins. History and legend ran wild around New Orleans—even more wild when that history and legend involved Captain Gabriel Dampier.

Nearly two centuries before, this swashbuckling privateer had secured his place in the local archives by supplying the city's aristocracy with not-entirely-legal supplies and merchandise to avoid paying the government's high tariffs on goods. He built the "hot" court for himself and his crew, a place to savor the delights of success before falling out of favor with polite society because of a debacle with a debutante.

But the captain had left behind his legacy in Court du Chaud, which still kept alive speculation about mysterious clues to hidden treasures, voodoo curses and haunted town houses. Josie had been born and raised here, but this morning, the familiar brick facades, iron-worked fences around neat squares of lawn and foliage seemed fresher and filled with promise.

Shutting the gate to her yard, she headed across the court to make her way down the alley, but instead of leaving, she crossed the patio of an open-air café, past tables draped in red holiday tablecloths. Café Eros connected her home to the exciting Quarter, the perfect blending of two worlds, past and present, private and public...no, Josie corrected herself, not public, but *welcoming.*

The café's owner, Chloe Matthews, was a woman who'd never met a stranger and, right now, Josie needed her friend's help to prepare for her special Christmas Eve guest.

A bell chimed to announce her entrance, and the door hadn't shut before Chloe waved her toward the counter. Weaving a path through tables, Josie glanced at a wall-sized mural of Captain Dampier, a swashbuckling figure who presided over the counter and kept alive the history of their notorious court. Chloe wasn't only a welcoming hostess and friend, but a clever businesswoman.

Mornings were always chaotic at Café Eros. Josie observed the customers...a businessman buried behind the newspaper's financial section, Claire and Randy from town houses twelve and thirteen with their heads bent low over a plate of sugary beignets. One of Court du Chaud's newer residents sat alone in the corner with his coffee—the dark and dangerous-looking man from Number 10.

This new neighbor didn't seem to notice her, probably wouldn't have noticed a Mardi Gras float if it squeezed through the front door and parked in the middle of the café.

He was too busy checking out Chloe.

Swallowing back a laugh, Josie made a mental note to pick her friend's brain about Number 10.

"Tell me I don't owe you more cookies this morning." Chloe sounded just breathless enough to convince Josie she was very aware of the man watching her.

"Tell me you're not complaining about the business."

Cocking an aproned hip against the counter, Chloe said, "I'd *never* complain about business. But I haven't met anyone as nuts about Christmas as you are."

"What's nuts?" Josie dropped her briefcase and leaned both elbows onto the counter to get a good look inside the display case. *Mmm.* As usual, all sorts of scrumptious, high-calorie goodies. "Christmas happens to be my favorite holiday."

"Got that part. You've had me baking since Thanksgiving."

"That really does sound like a complaint, but I'll forgive you for a cup of that divine-smelling French coffee."

Chloe headed toward the coffee machine, and by the time Josie got the first smooth, hot swallow down, she'd decided to cut her friend a break. Number 10 clearly had Chloe on edge.

"I need you to work your magic on *another* order," she said.

"Why am I not surprised? So what'll it be today? Honey balls for your boss or more surprise chocolate almond stockings for Madame Alain? Who, by the way, is trying to coerce me into revealing the identity of her secret Santa."

"You haven't told her it's me, have you?"

"Of course not. Client confidentiality."

"Priests, lawyers and bakers. Oh, my."

"Are you sure Nana LeClerc won't mind that you replaced her so quickly?"

"Absolutely not." Josie had played secret Santa to Max's grandmother ever since he'd left for college. She'd been too sad to stop after Nana's recent death. "I'm continuing the tradition in her honor."

"But you're continuing the tradition with *Madame Alain*. Nana LeClerc was a sweet old thing who never meddled in her neighbors' affairs."

Okay, Court du Chaud's resident busybody might not be the most obvious choice for her attentions... "You know Madame Alain is just as sweet. She's lonely. She lost her husband then Old Man Guidry and now Nana. She's the only one of Court du Chaud's old folks left. Nana would definitely approve."

"If you say so." Chloe shrugged. "So what's it going to be? And please don't tell me candy canes. Those little suckers require more concentration than I have right now."

Josie glanced at Number 10 in her periphery. No doubt. "No candy canes. I need a Café Eros special order. Remember those sugar cookies that you used to bake Nana to send her grandson, the cookies with the icing messages? I want an order of those. Only I want mine with *sexy* messages."

Chloe arched an eyebrow. "Just whom are you sending sexy messages to?"

"Number 17 himself."

"Nana's grandson?" Chloe demanded, referring to Max.

Josie nodded.

"The last I heard he'd only come back to take care of her things after the funeral. Sounds like you've been holding out on me, Josie Russell."

"Sounds like the pot is calling the kettle black, Chloe Matthews." She inclined her head toward the corner. "Unless Number 10 over there isn't aiming his X-ray vision at you."

"Shhh," she hissed.

Josie gave a laugh that drew the businessman's gaze above his newspaper.

Chloe scowled. "Sounds like we need a girls' night out."

"It's a date. I'll pencil you in right after Christmas." She glanced over at their neighbor from Number 12 and added, "We should invite Claire, too. She's looking pretty cozy with Number 13 over there. You sure you're not spiking the coffee with aphrodisiacs?"

"Weren't you the one who told me about the magic of Christmas?"

Josie laughed.

"Fine, I'll wait for all the juicy details, but you've got to give me something to hold me over. What's going on? Between work and your graduate classes, you barely look up long enough to smile at a guy let alone start up something with sexy cookies. And the last I heard, you were totally put out with this particular guy."

Sipping her coffee, Josie considered how best to respond. "I was put out with Max. Not only because he has been treating me like a stranger when we were practically raised together, but he didn't get home to say goodbye to Nana before she died."

"Josie, you said he tried, but he was halfway across the world when you called him."

"When I called his *personal assistant*. No one talks to Max LeClerc without getting through his posse nowadays. If it hadn't been for Nana and the business section of the newspaper, I wouldn't know a thing about him." She hadn't meant to sound quite so disapproving. But she had disapproved.

After college Max had headed into the world to seek his fortune. Now, as a venture capitalist, he traveled the globe, leading the sort of high-powered life that was light-years away from sultry, slow-paced Court du Chaud. Josie didn't care how he chose to live his life, but she thought he should have made more time for the woman who'd reared him. *A lot* more time.

Dear Nana had been old for as long as Josie had known her, and her passing at age ninety-two had been a peaceful one...except for her heartache at not seeing her grandson one last time. But Josie's anger at Max had yielded to real concern when she'd seen him at the funeral. There'd been something unexpected about him, something that struck her as so sad and...*lonely*.

She'd told herself she was being stupid. The young Max who she'd had a crush on had left all his human qualities behind when he'd gone off to college. The Max she read about in the newspaper's business section had grown into a ruthlessly ambitious man, who ate, drank and slept corporate takeovers.

That Max wouldn't be anything he didn't want to be, especially sad and lonely.

But Josie hadn't expected *that* Max to deal with his grandmother's possessions, either. She'd expected him to pass along the job to minions, to hop on his private jet and head into the bright blue beyond without a backward glance.

She'd been wrong. Max had surprised her by returning home a month after Nana's funeral. He hadn't left since.

"Have you asked the guy what's up?" Chloe asked.

"No. He's holed himself up inside Nana's place, and I've been playing hell trying to get him to come out."

Well, not *hell* exactly...

"So I ask again, how did we get from being put out with the guy to sexy Christmas cookies?" She dropped her voice to a whisper. "Are you trying to seduce him?"

Not *trying*. But she wasn't about to admit this in the middle of the café with customers in earshot, so Josie only smiled mysteriously, which her friend interpreted to mean yes.

"What about the bad blood between him and your brother?"

Josie had told Chloe all about how, once upon a time, Max and her brother Lucas had been the best of friends. "To this day my brother refuses to discuss the fight. Whatever happened was between him and Max. Not me. Madame Alain told me he's leaving right after Christmas. Thank goodness for her or I wouldn't have a clue what was going on. Since Lucas isn't due a visit until Mardis Gras, I don't see a conflict of interest, do you?"

Understanding dawned on Chloe's face, and she raised her hand for a high-five. "You go, girl. You've had a crush on this guy forever. Sounds like Santa sent you the perfect Christmas gift. It's about time you had some fun."

"Agreed." A fantasy night with Max would be the perfect break from her days spent running between her job as an assistant with social services and her classes at Tulane. "Can I swing by after work tomorrow to pick up my cookies?"

"Perfect. But just to clarify…you're officially trusting me to come up with your sexy messages?"

"Think romantic and tasteful. I'm assuming you named this place Café Eros for a reason."

"You know it," Chloe said. "And don't forget our girls' night out. I want the scoop."

Gulping down the last of her coffee, Josie darted a gaze at the man in the corner. "Me, too."

There was magic happening at Court du Chaud this Christmas.

She could *feel* it.

2

Number 17
Court du Chaud

MAX STOOD LOOKING out his front window long after Josie had left. Even without the briefcase, he knew she headed to work by the shapely length of hose-covered legs and stylish pumps exposed beneath the hem of her neat coat. She'd looked so professional and intent, a tantalizing stranger, and a smile played around his lips as he tried to reconcile the girl he'd once known with the woman who'd been playing very erotic games with him.

Since his return to Court du Chaud, Max had learned quite a few things about the woman Josie had grown to be. That she'd grown into such a beauty didn't surprise him. That she'd grown into a beauty willing to reach out and boldly take what she wanted did.

She'd surprised him most by wanting him.

Max remembered the first night he'd glanced across the alley to find her showcased in her bedroom window. The darkness outside had surprised him. He couldn't remember how much time had passed since he'd come upstairs to his grandmother's bedroom to sort through her personal things. What he'd found had been *seriously* personal. In her vanity, he'd found a stack of envelopes bound with gold ribbon, the paper brittle and yellowed with the years.

Love letters from his grandfather.

Curiosity about his grandparents had made him start reading, and he'd lost himself inside their lives as young lovers during a world war that had kept them apart.

He'd stayed in that wildly romantic place until soft light had reached across the alley to illuminate Josie, an unexpected vision of loveliness that had dragged him back to reality....

She was only a blur behind the white sheers. At first glance he recalled a lifetime of stories about ghosts that haunted the court, yet this woman was no ghost. He quickly recognized Josie, her slender body a smudge of shifting shadow as she moved around her bedroom, lifting her arms to unfasten her hair, shaking out the heavy mass.

He sat there, at first stunned then bedazzled by the sight of her behind those sheers, a filmy barrier that didn't shield as much as tantalize. He could imagine the shiny waves pouring over her shoulders, envision her eyes sparkling with excitement.

She moved to the dresser then stood before what he guessed was a mirror, drawing a brush through that silky mass with leisurely strokes, filling him with forbidden thoughts, making him imagine how her hair might feel in his hands.

He was struck by the intensity of his reaction, by how she breathed such promise into a simple task, each stroke a sensual play of motion and grace....

When she finally set down the brush and slipped open a dresser drawer to lift out clothing, she had him clutch-

ing the sides of the chair to keep anchored to the seat, resisting the urge to move to the window.

Then the sheers lifted on a night breeze. Suddenly Max could see Josie clearly. Raising her arms above her head, she pulled off a filmy camisole and gifted him with a perfect view of her breasts.

From this distance, he couldn't see details, couldn't know if her nipples gathered into tight peaks, but the sight rooted him to the spot, froze his breath as he waited for her to snap off the light and end the show.

But she just slipped off her skirt and began peeling away her hose. Then she bent over to pull on sexy shorts, treated him to a prime shot of her backside, and by the time she crawled into bed and turned off the light, his heart throbbed so hard, he thought it would explode. He should feel guilty for invading her privacy, but all he felt was grateful for the dazzling encounter that made him feel so alive....

Josie had become his lifeline in the darkness that night, salvation when he needed it most. From that moment forth, his days began blurring in anticipation of her nightly performances, making him finally face the reality of what his life had become.

Empty.

But reading his grandparents' letters and becoming involved with Josie had made him question the loneliness he'd felt for so long, made him understand how he'd cut himself off from everything really important in his life.

Now he stared into the court, acknowledging that *home* still felt familiar. Since his parents and grandfather had died in a boating accident when he was young, Max had been reared in his grandmother's home, becoming a part of Court du Chaud as if he'd been born here.

The Russell family next door at Number 16 had embraced him as much more than their son's best friend, too. They'd helped fund his way through private school and included him on family vacations. They'd become family, and after his fallout with Lucas, he'd needed to prove himself, to make good with his life so he felt worthy of their support and his grandmother's unwavering devotion.

He'd used his company's ranking on the stock exchange and his portfolio as the yardstick. He'd placed more importance on repaying the Russells' college loans and paying off his grandmother's mortgage and financial obligations than on staying involved with the people who'd cared about him.

He'd accomplished his goals, but had still gone on proving himself. It was only now, while sorting through the remnants of his grandmother's life, that he realized if given a choice, she'd have likely sacrificed financial security to see him more.

Max had made so many errors of judgment and only glimpsed the truth now that he let himself feel again. Josie's performances had breathed life back into him, and he'd begun questioning the decisions he'd made through the years.

For the first time in forever, he thought about the excitement he'd once felt on Christmas morning, racing down the stairs to see if Santa had visited during the night. He remembered the daring he'd always felt with Lucas as they dreamt up wild schemes to perpetrate the myth that a pirate ghost was cursed to haunt Court du Chaud forever.

He'd once felt *alive.*

Max wanted to grasp that feeling with both hands again, didn't want to waste another second when he'd already wasted so much time. He wanted to cross the alley, even knowing that taking this next step meant facing his past, and Lucas.

He owed that to Josie, and himself.

When the telephone rang a short time later, Max glanced at the display with a mixture of resignation and relief. It was still early in California, but he'd explained the importance of his business to an assistant when he'd made the call yesterday.

Taking a deep breath, Max steeled himself to face the man who'd once been like a brother. He had to resolve their past to make way for the future. Then he reached for the receiver. "Lucas, thanks for returning my call."

LA VEILLE DE NOËL. Notre nuit pour la fantaisie.

Christmas Eve. Our night for fantasy.

That was the response Josie had sent back to his invitation, so he'd spent his day planning a fantasy Christmas Eve. Tonight would be their first official night together, although he still found it ironic that after several weeks of corresponding and playing their intimate game, they still hadn't spoken beyond a few heartfelt condolences during his grandmother's services.

Lights twinkled in the foliage along her walkway, and Max felt more eager than ever before, an excitement that spurred him to take the porch steps two at a time. He thrust aside thoughts of the time when he'd run in and out of this town house as often as he had his own.

He'd already made the first move to make peace with Lucas, who'd laughed upon hearing that Max and Josie were interested in resuming a friendship.

"I never told my sister what caused our problem, so you

owe her an explanation," Lucas had said. *"Square things with Josie, and you've squared them with me. Then God help you, Max, because once my sister sets her mind on something, there's absolutely nothing she won't do to get it."*

Max wasn't sure what to make of that warning, but as the willing audience of Josie's steamy performances, he agreed with Lucas's assessment of her determination. He and Josie had a lot to talk about to bridge the distance across the alley, to clear away the past and make their relationship real.

When the door opened, Max found himself staring inside with an unexpected sense of longing. Yet it wasn't the house that struck such deep chords, but the woman who appeared, the coach lamp spilling light onto her face, a face both familiar yet new.

When he'd left Court du Chaud, Josie had been caught firmly between being a girl and a woman. She'd fulfilled her potential far beyond his expectations. Willowy and slender, the top of her head came right to his chin. Josie, the charming girl he'd once known, had grown to be the exquisitely beautiful woman he'd always known she would.

Max found his gaze locked onto every detail.... The way the light washed her chocolate hair with golden highlights, bathed her features in a glow that made her green eyes seem brighter, her pink mouth entirely kissable. And even more beautiful was her welcoming smile, a vibrant, easy smile that assured him she was as excited as he was.

Their shared past might never have been. Suddenly, all the intimacy they'd explored together, the letters filled with sexy requests and nights of erotic performances stretched between them. They were adults who'd covered a lot of ground together and were eager to cover more.

"Merry Christmas, Josie." Bringing her hands to his lips, he pressed a kiss to her soft skin, touching her. *Finally.* Her hands were warm, satin smooth and the moment became surreal with her taste on his mouth, her scent on his breath.

"Merry Christmas, Max."

Her smile sparkled in her eyes, and she was a vision in cream lace, some ultrafeminine dress both flowy and clingy in a way that made him notice all her curves. He couldn't help lingering over her hands. A blush colored her cheeks, and he knew she felt the moment as intensely as he.

Once they might have been friends, but now they were almost strangers with bare skin and an alley between them.

"Come on in." The words broke from her lips in a breathy burst, and her hands slipped from his as she stepped back into the foyer.

Moving inside, he waited while she closed the door and swept past, unable to keep his gaze from skimming over all that flowy lace. He could envision her long legs below, had seen those shapely legs bared in her window, had fantasized about peeling away her hose and touching all her creamy skin.

His night had finally arrived.

She swept a hand toward the living room, which was filled with so many poinsettias and red roses the place might have been a floral warehouse. "All right, I have to ask. How did you load up my house with all these gorgeous flowers? I keep a spare key outside, but not in the same place my parents did."

"I want to keep that a secret for right now, if you don't mind." He'd get around to telling her about his conversation with Lucas, once they'd had a chance to talk.

"I love secrets. And surprises. I was completely surprised when I walked in the door after work. I've never seen my place so Christmas-y, and that's saying a lot."

It was indeed. Josie's decorations went far beyond a decorated tree. A winter village complete with snow-topped hills and houses with twinkling lights in the windows. A nativity scene displayed on the fireplace mantel, and a Santa laughed in his sleigh while reindeer carried him up the balustrade toward the town house's second floor.

"I like what you've done around here," he said. "It's different than I remember."

"My parents expected me to go off to college like Lucas. They wanted to retire to Florida, so I talked them into selling me the house then remodeled it to make it mine."

Max glanced at the buff-colored walls and elaborate rattan furniture with deep, plush cushions. A decor that was homey and welcoming yet whimsical. Very Josie.

"But you didn't want to leave New Orleans."

"No place like it."

"Have you traveled much?" he asked. "My grandmother told me you stuck close to home with college and work."

"I don't have to travel to know New Orleans is special, Max. It's home. How could any place be like it?"

There was nothing in her tone to make her words an admonishment, but his own nagging guilt made them feel that way. He didn't get a chance to reply before she continued.

"You'll have to tell me how New Orleans holds up against all the exciting places you've visited. I've read about how you jet-set around the world."

"You've *read* about me?"

She nodded. "In the business section. There are tidbits

about you in there all the time. What corporation you're gobbling up. What evasive maneuvers CEOs are taking to steer out of your path. That sort of thing."

"I didn't know you were so interested in business."

"I'm not. I'm interested in you." She eyed him like a temptress. "I have to tell you I'm surprised, though. I've read all you do is work, but you've been home for a month now. How does someone as busy as you manage so much time off work?"

"Owning the company helps," he said dryly, not entirely sure what to make of her admission. "I'm considering an organizational restructure right now. I'm in the process of deciding whether to buy out my partner and downsize the firm."

"Really? I haven't read one word about that. You must be keeping it hush-hush from the media."

"You're one of the illustrious few to share in the big company secret."

"I'm flattered. And surprised again."

"Why?"

"Downsizing seems inconsistent with the fast track you've been on."

"Do you believe everything you read about me in the business section?"

"Of course not, but Nana always said you planned to take over the world."

Max heard the echo of his grandmother's pride, which only reminded him that he hadn't found time to share with her. Ten years had been a drop in the bucket in her long life, but those had been years they could have spent together. He'd distanced himself even more from the Russell family.

Ten years constituted a significant portion of his life,

and he'd spent those years cut off from the people who'd loved him. But no more.

He'd learned his lesson the hard way.

Sliding a bloom from a vase, Max held it to Josie, and when she reached out, he skimmed the dewy petals along her fingers, a reminder that he'd been watching her, *wanting* her, and was now finally, *finally* close enough to touch.

"You've done so much to make every night memorable since I came back to Court du Chaud, Josie. You've pleased me very much. Now I have a chance to please you." Another graze of those dewy petals across her fingers.

"Welcome home, Max."

Brushing the rose against her mouth, he traced her lush lips, inspired by her reaction. Her tongue darted out in the wake of his touch, and he watched, the promise of sex swelling between them, no longer a faraway fantasy, but exquisitely real.

She inhaled a breath that made her chest rise sharply, and it was then Max noticed the silver chain around her neck.

Dipping his gaze toward the swell of creamy breasts, he recognized the filigreed angel nestled in her cleavage and wondered that she treasured such a small gift when, according to Lucas, she still didn't know who'd sent it.

"We have a lot to talk about." When he lifted his gaze from that swell of creamy skin, he found her smile fading away. Her gaze narrowed, and the moment was broken.

"Why am I not surprised?"

He slid the rose back into a vase. "About what?"

"You wanting to *talk*."

"You don't think that's where we should start?"

Leaning up on tiptoe, she moved close enough to whisper in his ear. "Max, we've already started."

That sultry voiced reminder whipped through him with the force of a level five hurricane. He had to swallow hard to find his voice. "True. But we need to establish where to go next since we're going about things in an unusual order."

"Backward?"

"No. We've known each other all our lives. But we have history that needs to be dealt with. We're moving in a new direction without knowing what we want from each other."

"Notre nuit pour la fantaisie." She slipped her fingers around his neck.

Her whole body melted toward him as she pulled him just close enough so they nearly touched, and his breath stalled when she whispered, "The whole point of a fantasy night is that it's just one night. No past. No family. No reality. Just you and me right now."

Right now his blood pumped into the red zone, making it tough to think. He could only stare into her beautiful face, into eyes so bright they seemed alive with green fire.

"You don't know what I want from you."

She nodded, sending sleek waves tumbling sexily around her shoulders. "You want to touch me. You said so in your letter."

That sparked a few brain cells and cued him that there was more happening here than he knew. But Max couldn't figure out what, not with her warm curves tantalizing him with each rise and fall of her breasts.

"I do want to touch you. I think you know how much." Placing a finger beneath her chin, he willed her to see how deeply he meant what he said, how seriously he took *them*.

"I want to make up for lost time," he admitted. "I want to know all about the beautiful woman you've grown up to be. I want to know if you're wearing your hair down because I wrote that I liked it. I want to know if you're wearing the lingerie I sent beneath your pretty dress."

He lifted her chin higher and leaned forward to whisper in her ear. "I want to know how much you want me."

She trembled, a full-bodied motion that belied her bold look. "Yes, I'm wearing my hair down for you, Max, but I won't tell you what's under my dress. That's a surprise."

Stepping out of his reach with a jaunty toss of her head, she left him staring after her with his heart pounding too hard. "We'll talk if that's what you want. May I get you something to drink first?"

"I put a bottle of wine in your fridge."

"Thanks. I haven't made it into the kitchen yet. I was too busy dressing to entice you into undressing me."

She took off toward the kitchen, her backside swaying under all that creamy silk. He forced his feet into motion to follow, to grab wineglasses from the china cabinet.

She met him in the dining room, and he opened the bottle and poured, then cornered her against the table to press a glass into her hand. "A toast, Josette."

"To Christmas?"

"To us." Tapping his glass to hers, he met her gaze over the rim. "To finding things where we didn't expect them."

"I'm glad you found me, Max."

"Me, too."

Bringing the glass to her lips, she sipped, a move he followed with his gaze. The possibilities of the night ahead turned each sip into a visual feast of moist lips, darting tongues and the promise of sex. The moment was exciting and tentative. This was all so new between them.

"What made you perform for me that first night?"

She eyed him over her glass. "I saw you across the alley and was just annoyed enough to want a reaction."

"Annoyed? Why?"

"Because you were unfriendly. I talked to you at Nana's service then you left town without saying goodbye and came back without saying hello. You've been holed up inside your place night and day. Madame Alain has been the only person you've chatted with."

And not because he'd been in the chatting mood. But to explain why he'd holed up inside his place would mean explaining how far he'd traveled from Court du Chaud in the years since he'd left and how he'd been reevaluating every choice he'd made. Now wasn't the time for confessions, not when he was trying to figure out what she wanted.

"I'm sorry, Josie. I—"

Lifting her fingers to his mouth, she stopped him with a touch, pressed until he could taste her warm skin on a breath. "No apology necessary. We've moved past reality, remember? We're all about fantasy now."

He caught her wrist and watched, satisfied, as her eyes widened in surprise. Then he lifted her hand so he could trail an openmouthed kiss down her fingers, along her palm.

Josie sighed.

"Is that all that you want from me? A fantasy?"

"I want you to touch me. That's what you said you wanted, too. Or would you rather *talk?*" She turned her face enough to brush those velvet lips against his fingers. "What else is there for us, Max? You're only home for a visit. I think this is the perfect opportunity to explore how we feel."

"What about Lucas?"

"My brother doesn't belong in bed with us."

Max chuckled softly. "Agreed, but he's between us in or out of bed. I'd rather deal with him up front."

"Whatever happened between you and Lucas is over. I'm not interested in reality when we can enjoy a fantasy."

"You want to keep our involvement a secret?"

"If you haven't noticed, I'm the only one left in New Orleans. I don't usually call my family to announce every man I get involved with." She waved a hand dismissively. "And what would be the point? Madame Alain told me you were leaving right after Christmas. I respect the kind of life you lead now, Max. I know you date high-powered corporate women who aren't looking for commitments. I don't have any problem with that. Tonight can be our denouement."

"You read about my dates in the business section?"

"No, the society column. They cover all those corporate fund-raisers. I want you to know that I can play by the rules. Let's just enjoy our night. No Lucas, no parents, no strings. When you're ready to leave town, I'll blow you a kiss and say *au revoir*. We'll both have enjoyed our time together and have some really great memories."

It took a moment for her proposal to register. Josie thought she understood the way he operated.

The kicker…she did.

At least the way he'd operated until he'd returned home to start taking stock of his life.

"We're both consenting adults who know the rules." She extended her hand. "So what do you say? Want to shake and seal the deal?"

Notre nuit pour la fantaisie.

Looked as though Josie wasn't interested in reality at all, which meant Max now had a problem.

There was no place for temporary in his seduction. He wanted Josie more than he'd ever wanted anyone before and temporary wouldn't work when her family and the past still lay between them. Not to mention his promise to Lucas to come clean.

So Max didn't shake to conclude their transaction, but drew her toward him until she pressed those sleek curves close and was forced to tip her head back to meet his gaze.

"Actually, Josie, I'd rather kiss you."

He'd have to convince her she wanted more than one night, and he had only one night to convince her.

3

MAX'S HUNGRY EXPRESSION might have been straight from Josie's imagination, but when he lowered his face to hers, he was no longer a fantasy. Her mouth parted instinctively, and, in a whole-bodied motion, she pressed herself against him, wrapped her arms around his neck, felt every inch of his hard body against hers.

His hands were suddenly on her, too, fingers threading through her hair, anchoring her head so he could slant his mouth across hers to deepen their kiss.

Their tongues tangled. Their breaths collided. But it was the strength of his hunger that stole her breath.

This man was passion…*want*. His kiss wasn't all the steamy fun fantasy she'd expected but an intense hunger that sexy performances and provocative gift-giving had honed to a fine edge.

He kissed her as if he'd waited forever for the privilege, as if he was determined to overwhelm her and shut out everything in her world except for him.

And he did.

Josie could still envision the expression on his handsome face, even though her eyes had long since closed. She tasted his warm mouth, stole his breath and offered hers in return.

This was the Max of her fantasies, the object of her desires for as far back as she could remember. A little older and a lot sexier.

Threading her fingers into his hair, she anchored him close and hung on, her own need an ache inside, fueling a desire that had waited to be satisfied for so long.

She drank in the taste of his mouth against hers, the way their tongues tangled together hungrily, each sexy stroke stirring a reply deep inside. She could feel him everywhere as he skimmed his hands down the curve of her neck, molded her shoulders, moved down her back with complete freedom.

Arching against him, she invited him to explore to his heart's content, thrilled to finally get on with their night and didn't become aware of the knocking until he groaned, a low rumble that tasted of needy male and sounded like pure frustration.

"Dinner," he whispered against her mouth when the knocking grew more insistent.

His mouth lingered on hers until she gathered her wits enough to let him loose. Then he stepped away and all she could do was stare back as his warm gaze poured over her, a look of possessive male.

She watched him head to the door, taking in his broad shoulders, trim waist and very nice butt. He looked so different from the man who'd returned home not so long ago, and Josie liked the changes. His clean business haircut had gone the way of his custom-tailored suits, and sometime during the weeks between the services and packing up Nana's things, his hair had filled in enough to wave at his nape.

The man she'd been reading about had been on the fast track to a heart attack. Making time to relax and have some fun had done him good, she decided.

A night of fantasy would do him one better.

When two waiters from Commodore Pete's seafood restaurant marched into her house, Josie retreated into the living room. She turned on a sultry jazz version of Christmas tunes and dimmed all the lights until only the tree and the winter village lit the shadows with jeweled brilliance.

Pleased by the effect, she half sat on the edge of the sofa and listened to Max giving directions to the waiters, who proceeded to create a candlelit fantasy dinner for two in her dining room.

He hadn't missed a trick to make their night together special, and that fluttery place deep inside thrilled with excitement for the night ahead. She smiled when the waiters finally headed past her with polite nods.

Max saw them out and returned. "Hungry?"

"Starved. But I had no idea Commodore Pete delivered. It usually takes weeks to get a reservation at his place."

"Does it? Pete's an old friend from school."

She nodded, liking that he'd made contact with someone else from his past, another connection to home after such a long time away. Nana would have been pleased, too.

"So I chose well?" He extended his hand, and she slipped her fingers into his, let him lead her to the table.

"Absolutely. With school and work, I never know what I'm doing from one minute to the next, let alone long enough ahead to book a reservation at Commodore Pete's. The only time I go is when my boss Courtney takes me out for my annual birthday dinner. I think she's a friend of his, too."

"She obviously knows how much you love seafood."

"You remembered?"

He nodded, and the knowing look in his gaze made the

years between the past and the present melt like sugar on a hot beignet. They'd known each other so well, and that knowledge translated into a comfort level that let them segue easily into provocative performances and sexy gifts.

Now that knowledge would span the alley.

They sat down to a meal that typified all the yummy reasons why Commodore Pete had a backlist for tables, and chatted about routine things while they ate. Her family. His work. New York where he based his firm. New Orleans and how much it had changed in the past ten years.

He was the Max she remembered. He smiled easily and made her laugh with his dry observations about life. Compared to her control-freak brother, he'd always been the more laid-back of the pair, the one who could go with the flow.

Talking with him brought back so many memories, reminded her of why she'd always been so enamored. He'd put his charm to good use in his fast-track social life according to the newspaper, and he put that charm to work now.

After the baked oysters "la Louisiane" and crab chops "à la nouvelle," Josie was practically bursting to get on with their night and claim another kiss.

They'd caught up so the past was officially over and all they had to think about was *now*.

"I hope you saved some room for dessert." She finally slipped away from the table and headed to the Christmas tree where she'd left a package.

Max sat back in his chair and eyed her curiously.

"A Christmas gift." She presented him with a string-tied box.

"Thank you."

Kneeling before him, Josie spread out her skirt and trailed her gaze up the well-toned terrain of his body. He untied the string, lifted the box top and peered in at the neatly layered sugar cookies inside.

"Nana always baked you those big sugar cookies and wrote love notes in icing for every holiday," she said softly. "I didn't want this to be your first Christmas without them."

He arched an eyebrow. "Love notes? She wrote *messages* on them."

"Pshaw. If they weren't *love* notes, you wouldn't have been so stingy with them."

"I shared."

"Only the broken ones."

He laughed, and she felt a thrill skitter through her when he caressed her with his deep gaze.

"I recognize this box. These are the same cookies my grandmother had been sending me lately," he said. "I guessed she wasn't baking them herself, but I didn't want to ask."

Josie couldn't miss the way he softened around the edges and slipped her hand over his. For quite some time, she'd been the one placing the orders at Café Eros and mailing the packages at Nana's request, ever since getting around had become too difficult and tiring for Nana.

"Wait a second...." Max poked around inside. "These are *not* the same cookies. My grandmother never sent me any cookie that said *undress me*. This one says—Undress *For* Me."

When he laughed, Josie dared a peek inside the box to find a cookie bearing two simple numbers in scrolling red and green icing that read the same whether she viewed it right side up or upside down....

"My pleasure." He captured her gaze with a look that was all naughty male.

Her belly swooped wildly in reply, and she couldn't decide if she should kiss or kill Chloe. She'd placed an order for romantic and tasteful cookies, not *X-rated.*

But X-rated did seem to be moving things along. And when Josie got down to it, who was she to argue with a woman who'd made a career of whipping up sexy recipes for her clients?

"Since you've given me my gift, Josette, I'm going to enjoy it." He held up a cookie that read: Dance With Me. "Not to be confused with 'Dance *For* Me,' which I was hoping you'd do for me tonight, too. That's my fantasy."

Her breath fluttered crazily inside, a reaction to the promise in his words and the sound of her full name in that hint-of-the-Deep-South drawl. "You've been busy. Between spending your nights staring into my bedroom window and writing sexy letters and shopping for all my lovely gifts, when did you have time to fantasize?"

Sliding his chair back, he stood and drew her to her feet. "You'd be surprised at how much time I've found to fantasize about you."

And as he led her out of the dining room, there was something so earnest about him that Josie didn't doubt his claim for a second. She was *his* fantasy and found irony tasted as sweet as Chloe's cookies.

He slipped his arms around her and fitted her against him more perfectly than imagination could have ever allowed, his cheek against her temple, fingers twined, thighs brushing. His groin grazed her as they moved, a suggestive heat that proved he was affected by their closeness, too.

She exhaled a satisfied sigh and pressed her face to his shoulder. With each breath, she enjoyed his scent, the crisp smell of his shirt, the warm male ambrosia of the skin below.

Her body rode softly against his as they moved to the sultry music, his touch guiding her in their dance.

"Tell me about your fascination with Christmas." He brushed her hair with a kiss and the moment took on a dreamlike quality with the sound of his throaty voice and the multihued Christmas lights twinkling. "I've always known how much you loved it, but I can't remember ever hearing why."

"No special reason, really. The season of hope and promise and tradition. I just love the magic of it all."

"So you believe in magic?"

"Of course, don't you?" How could she answer otherwise while standing in his arms?

"Once."

That one word summed up all his years away from Court du Chaud. Suddenly, the life he'd been living didn't seem as fast or glamorous as the business section made it out to be. Josie was struck again by that same sense of loneliness she'd felt in him that first night he'd shown up in Nana's bedroom, and she wanted to reassure him that magic did exist. She could prove it—she'd been living out her fantasy for weeks now with him across the alley.

She wanted him to know that he still had someone who cared, but Josie wouldn't admit to her girlhood crush. That was a secret from her past, and she'd insisted on keeping the past out of their fantasy. Tonight was their night alone. No family, nothing but the two of them. "Maybe you've just forgotten, Max. You've been gone a long time."

"You think the magic has to do with being here."

"Court du Chaud is magic in a lot of ways, you know that. Not only do we have history, voodoo curses and ghosts, but being surrounded by people who love you is magical, too. You work so much that you haven't been home in too long."

"I thought you didn't believe everything you read in the paper."

"I believe what I see." She resisted the urge to glance up, didn't want him to glimpse any disapproval for the choices he'd made. "If it's any consolation, I've been accused of the same thing and couldn't deny it. Losing Nana and seeing you again has had me looking at my own life. That's one of the reasons I decided to dance for you that night. I knew you weren't home for long, so I didn't want to let the opportunity pass."

"*And* you were annoyed with me."

She smiled into his shirt. "And that."

"So what does that make me, Josette? A Christmas gift? Or a New Year's resolution? Are you turning over a new leaf to spend more time having fun?"

A new leaf? Chloe thought she needed to turn over a new one, but Josie hadn't thought much about her personal life until Max had come home. She hadn't had time.

Her career with social services was a passion, and that passion crept into her free time, too. She hoped to step into her boss's position as the president of the local Big Buddies chapter once Courtney's term ended. Right now she was the president of Krewe du Chaud and the homeowner's association, too. As soon as the new year began, school would start, and she'd wrap up her graduate program to start working on her doctorate.

She'd been as focused on work as she'd accused Max of being, and when she stood wrapped in his arms, their bodies moving with a rhythm like a slow bayou breeze, suddenly all her wonderfully exciting plans seemed part of a picture missing a big piece, a future that wasn't complete.

With a sigh, she rubbed her cheek against his shoulder, reminded herself that she had only one night with this man. She might need to consider turning over a new leaf, but she could sort out her life issues on her own time, *after* Max left.

The clock was ticking on her fantasy night.

4

"JOSIE, TELL ME—"

"Shh." Josie came to a stop, forcing Max to do the same. Raising up on tiptoes, she lifted her face to his and whispered against his lips. "I don't want to talk anymore—"

Catching her mouth in a hard kiss, he obliged. Their breaths clashed for an instant before Josie gave a pleasured sigh and arched against him, unable to resist the way he kissed her with such calm thoroughness, the way that sweet ache inside came alive. She wanted to feel him everywhere, wanted to savor every second of their night together. Just the two of them.

His tongue thrust possessively to tangle with hers, and she met each stroke. Exploring. Devouring. Now that the freedom to touch him was finally hers, she slipped her arms around his waist, dragged her hands up his back, discovered the strength of toned muscles and broad shoulders.

The Max of her fantasies.

As she traveled the taut muscles, learned the feel of him by touch, Josie knew he must still make time to work out. The business section might place him in boardrooms and on private jets, but the man she held in her arms found time to stay in shape.

Incredible shape.

She wondered if he worked out while talking business in a fancy club. Or on the golf course. Or while playing polo.

She didn't ask. She didn't see the point in chatting no matter how much she wanted to know about his life. He was leaving, and she'd soon be back to reading about him.

Until then she needed to savor the feel of his hands on her, the way his broad chest and strong arms blocked out the sight of everything but him. Tonight was hers. She'd seduced him fair and square and didn't want to waste a second.

Not when Max broke away to trail his mouth along her jaw. He rained openmouthed kisses in that sensitive hollow behind her ear. He dragged his lips down her neck, and her pulse thudded hard in reply as he explored every inch of her skin, testing, tasting, igniting a fiery reply deep inside.

And she wasn't the only one affected. She recognized his ragged breaths, his chest rising and falling sharply. His grip tightened as if he clung to his control, as if she made him feel raw around the edges.

Dragging her hands down his waist, she molded the tight curve of his butt, nudging him closer to gauge the physical effect she was having on him.

A *very* physical effect.

A length of impressive erection suddenly nestled against her belly, and Josie couldn't resist rocking back and forth in welcome. Parting her legs, she rode his thigh, a long stroke that caught her in just the right place. Max gave a throaty growl, and their fantasy officially started.

They stood in the glow of dazzling Christmas lights

making out as if they'd waited forever. And they had. Every night of provocative performances and every morning of sexy letters and gifts had mounted the tension to the breaking point.

They didn't have to waste time with the preliminaries of getting to know each other. They'd known each other forever, and although Max had been gone a while, he was still Max. Trustworthy. Gorgeous. Oh-so yummy.

So Josie concentrated on capturing each moment in memory, the feel of her cheek against his shirt, the warm muscle below. His thigh nudging between hers as he led her in their dance. The sweet ache that pooled low in her belly. The want that was more exquisite than she'd ever imagined.

The promise of the night ahead.

She'd barely caught her breath by the time she realized Max was maneuvering them toward the table. It took another moment to discover what he was after.

The cookies.

Holding her tucked firmly against him with one arm, he flipped open the box.

"Here it is." He held up a cookie.

Dance for me.

He took a big bite.

Laughing, Josie rose on tiptoes to kiss a crumb from his mouth. Then she caught his hand and dragged him back into the living room to the sofa. "You sit and I'll dance."

His smile was all male. And while he'd always been beautiful with his tawny golden looks and deep blue eyes, life and maturity had hardened his features, sculpted the strong angles of his face, honed beautiful into striking.

Max settled in comfortably for the show. Her heart rate

spiked hard, and she felt the heat in his gaze. She turned away and headed across the room, steeling her nerves for the performance ahead.

There was no denying that *imagining* Max watching was an entirely different experience than *facing* Max while he watched.

She could see expectation on his face, practically feel excitement radiating off him like the summer sun on hot pavement. She breathed deeply to center herself, to rally her boldness, to let that indulged expression on his face provoke her. To dare. To want. She wanted hunger to sharpen his features, wanted to see him struggle with his control.

She wanted to dazzle him with desire.

He'd sent her lacy undergarments, and the card tucked inside his gift had expressed how much he would enjoy knowing she wore his gift during the day while she worked. Josie had done as he'd asked. She'd savored the feel of the soft lace under her suit, while sexy thoughts of him back in Number 17 had distracted her all day.

Tonight she'd worn his sexy undies again and would treat him to an up close and personal glimpse of just how sexy those thoughts had been.

Closing her eyes, she focused on the music, let the smooth notes pour through her. She began a simple swaying that loosened her muscles and made her feel decadent.

Working the buttons at her throat, she slipped each through its hole, a thoughtful unveiling of skin and the camisole below. The lace caressed her skin with every move, tantalizing her with a soft touch, arousing her with thoughts of pleasing Max.

Just slipping the sleeves down her arms became an

erotic dance, and she dragged the blouse around her neck, along her shoulders, showcasing the camisole, which had cups that precluded the need for any bra.

The lift-and-separate action displayed her cleavage to amazing advantage. She dipped forward to give him a shot through the tangle of her long hair. She chanced a peek at him to find the look she'd imagined so often in her fantasies—his strong face sharpening with his need to touch her.

Je t'ai regardée. Je t'ai désirer. Maintenant je veux te toucher.

Slowly she shimmied closer, not wanting him to miss a thing, her movements emboldened by one simple desire—making Max want her more than he'd ever wanted before.

All those high-powered women in his life might suit the corporate shark he'd become, but he was back in Court du Chaud now. Here they played life by different rules. The days slowed to a sultry Louisiana pace, a pace meant to endure the heat, and to savor pleasure.

She wanted him to remember this night, so when he returned to his fast-track life, he wouldn't find it so easy to forget his roots. She didn't want him to forget her, or the woman she'd grown up to be. She wanted a place in his memory all to herself, wanted him to recall her whenever he thought of home, wanted him to burn when he did.

So she let the blouse slide from her fingers, draped it across his lap, where a telltale bulge proved she was on her way to getting her wish even though her performance had only begun.

The dark expanse across their alley had always hidden Max's responses. Her imagination had made her bold, but now, seeing the tautness of his well-toned body and watching his fingers dig into the sofa…Josie hadn't known how empowering she'd find this man in his desire. His want fueled her own. Her body responded to the sight of him as if she'd waited forever.

She had.

With a smile, she met his gaze and reached for the fastening at her waist. His eyes sparkled with anticipation, then slipped away as she rocked her hips back and forth in a seductive motion, turning around as she worked the lined skirt down, down, down…. She let it fall to the floor.

Now he knew what was under her skirt.

His camisole with silky garter straps. Thigh-high hose. No panties, but lots and lots of bare skin. Now he knew she'd sat across from him during dinner, she'd danced in his arms with all her intimate places caressing the skirt's soft lining.

Max liked what he saw.

He grazed his hand across her bottom when she danced close, just a brush of warm fingers that conveyed his need like a current across her skin. Slipping his fingers between her thighs, he teased her moist folds, a tantalizing touch that made her sex give a single hard throb in reply.

"You have no idea how much I want to touch you, Josette. All of you."

But she did know. Want was all over his heavy-lidded expression. His voice was a raw ache, a needy sound that made her smile.

"And you will. *Soon.*"

She didn't know how much longer she could wait, either. She felt more decadent than she'd ever dreamed possible while standing before him in her sexy outfit that revealed so much more skin than it concealed.

A trembling excitement built deep inside, fueled by his hungry expression, by his sense of eagerness. A man whose patience had almost reached an end. His struggle not to shove out of the sofa and grab her was all over him.

Goose bumps washed over her bare skin, a physical display of her arousal when he skimmed those fingertips behind her knee, a glancing touch that sent another current through her.

But their show wasn't over just yet, and laughing, she sauntered out of reach, twirling in time with the heady beat, teased by the way her nipples caressed the lace. Sliding a hand over her tummy, Josie circled slowly before him, gifting him with her swaying hips, her bare bottom, and after a complete revolution, she aimed her fingers toward her thighs.

She touched herself where he'd just touched her. She tempted him with all that could be his now that he'd crossed the alley to join her fantasy. Arching her back, she thrust forward her breasts brazenly, flaunted nipples that jabbed eagerly against the lace, and brought her long hair into the dance.

She meant to tease him, but it was her body that burned each time her hair swished across her waist, every part of her skin so sensitized. She could practically feel his gaze cut across the jeweled darkness, his eyes burning with a heat she could now finally see.

The reality of him watching—*wanting*—thrilled the places where she touched herself, made her knees weak. Which meant this dance had to come to an end. Collapsing into a boneless heap at this man's knees wasn't on tonight's program.

Josie planned to bring Max to his knees.

* * *

MAX'S BREATH CAUGHT in his throat when Josie sauntered near, all sleek curves, creamy skin and sultry grace. She rose above him in a glorious display of sensuous woman, and before he could rally enough brain cells to react, he found her straddling him, hose-clad knees sliding along his legs, the sleek expanse of parted thighs spread across his lap.

She planted her hands on the sofa behind him, filling his vision with the sight of full breasts swelling over her bodice, long shiny hair playing peek-a-boo with all her curves.

"Ah, Josie—"

"Shh, no talking." She dropped a kiss to his lips. "No thinking. Just let yourself feel, and enjoy."

No problem. He wanted to feel every inch of this warm temptress, and when she started moving seductively in a lap dance straight from a wild dream, Max felt, and enjoyed.

Slipping his hands behind her, he cupped her backside, followed her sultry rhythm as his body temperature soared. She stretched out above him, while his gaze hungrily traveled up every inch of that gorgeous terrain, all glossy dark hair, bare skin and soft lace, until the seam biting into his crotch was the only thing keeping him from dragging her onto the couch and underneath him.

He dug his fingers into her sweet cheeks, lifting her on each upstroke enough to glimpse all the secrets hiding within the neatly trimmed hair between her thighs. When she spread wider to accommodate him, suddenly all those warm folds lined up with his erection. Max could feel her heat through his pants, felt himself grow impossibly harder.

"Josie," he ground out in a stranger's voice.

He couldn't stop from lifting his hips to ride the ache, to press against all her soft places and imagine the feel of skin against skin. She breathed his name on a sigh when her body met his in a breathtaking collision.

Stunned by the intensity of his reaction, he couldn't remember ever wanting the way he wanted Josie, could barely think beyond wondering how he'd managed to withstand her determined seduction for so long.

How he'd resist her now that she rode him with luxurious strokes.

Working his way along her body, Max distracted himself by the feel of silky hose along her thighs, skidded his palms past the hose and up bare skin to the smooth expanse of her lace covered stomach.

Josie trembled, one of those all-over shivers that told him she felt his touch everywhere. And this was exactly the distraction he needed. Dragging his hands up her ribs, he lowered his face to her breasts and caught the lace on her bodice with his teeth.

Her chest rose and fell on a sharp breath as he tugged the whole thing down. Her breasts spilled out, assaulting him with the tempting softness of her skin, an innocently seductive vanilla scent that was hers alone.

His hands tightened around her waist as he absorbed the incredible sight of her. She swayed her hips in a hypnotic, erotic motion. Her creamy breasts thrust upward temptingly, puckered nipples begging him to lean forward and taste.

He couldn't resist. No way.

Lifting his gaze, Max watched her as he sucked a taut tip into his mouth, tasted her warm skin. Her lips parted around a tiny whimper, a pouty, kissable moue, as she tossed her head back, hair tumbling behind her shoulders in a sleek wave.

Catching the other tip between his thumb and forefinger, he tugged lightly, smiling when she slid her hands over his shoulders to brace herself against another shiver. The sight of her burned through him. He liked discovering what aroused her, and made love to her beautiful breasts until she exhaled his name on a sigh and pressed against him, trying to knead her orgasm into breaking.

She was too close to kneading *his* into breaking.

So easing his fingers between them, Max touched her intimately, sought that tiny bundle that centered the core of her pleasure.

"Oh, Max…" she cried out when he found it.

Exploring her with a familiarity that made his mouth go dry, he brought her to climax with deliberate strokes, the promise of greater pleasures to come.

Because that's what he wanted from Josie.

More than one night of pleasure.

5

JOSIE EXHALED a series of shuddering gasps and dissolved against him, an enticing armful of warm skin and satisfied sighs. Max took advantage of the moment, nestling her close, amazed by how right she felt.

He knew this feeling. In business it translated into the moment he was on the brink of a conquest, when his wheeling and dealing came together and all the pieces fell into place.

He'd learned what he needed to know, what he wanted for the future.

Josie.

As if she could sense his thoughts, she nuzzled her face against his neck, made him wish he was naked everywhere. "I wanted to bring *you* to your knees."

"You've been doing that every night for weeks now. Fair's fair. It was my turn."

She laughed softly. "I'd forgotten how you did that."

"What?"

"Always said the right thing."

"Did I?"

"Mmm-hmm. Now don't get me wrong. You could still be a nightmare, but that was usually because of Lucas. When you were on your own, you were always decent."

"I don't guess you've been reading about how decent I am in the business section."

"Hardly. According to the press, you're as cutthroat as our pirate captain."

Was it any wonder Josie hadn't considered he could offer her any more than a fling?

The answer was so obvious it ached. She'd been judging him by what his grandmother shared and by what she read. She had every right to expect him to avail himself of their time together then leave town without a backward glance.

He'd earned that reputation.

He traced her spine beneath her glossy hair, willed her to see past the man he'd become.

"I hope you'll give me a chance to prove I can be more than my press, Josette."

"You think I don't know that already?"

"I haven't been home in a long time."

"You're still you, Max."

Something in her expression assured him she would have never involved herself in their erotic game if she hadn't believed that about him.

He liked her honesty, and her boldness. She was beautifully comfortable in her seminudity, and he ran his hands down her arms, thumbed her nipples just to watch her respond. He reached for the necklace dangling between her breasts.

"Isn't it lovely?" she asked. "It was a Christmas gift from a long time ago."

Max already knew, but suddenly he wanted to hear why she still wore that tiny angel. *Needed* to. "Tell me."

"It was a gift from my first secret Santa. Someone who

was kind to me when I needed kindness. I've always valued that, so I wear this to remind me." For a moment her stare was as deep as the bayou at sunset, shadowy, still, and somehow sad. Then it was gone, and her grin flashed bright. "I was so inspired that I still keep up the tradition."

"Really?" Lucas hadn't mentioned this. "With whom?"

"Every year I coordinate the name swap in my office, but Nana was the first person I ever played secret Santa for, and for the longest, incidentally. I'm sure she knew it was me, but I never officially fessed up. Not once in all these years."

She looked so pleased with herself, and she had every right to be. Her love of Christmas and belief in its magic infected everyone around her. His grandmother had always known how giving Josie was, and while Max might have forgotten in the years he'd been away, he'd been feeling the effects of her special attention ever since his return.

Reaching up, he thumbed her lower lip, craving a touch of her soft smile. "My grandmother never told me she had a secret Santa, but I'm sure she enjoyed having one. She loved you."

Her eyes fluttered shut, lashes fringing in semicircles on her cheeks. She exhaled a warm breath against his fingers. "We're doing it again."

"What?"

"Talking. It's my turn, Max."

"To get me on my knees?"

"Mmm-hmm." And as she said it, she scooted off his lap, the silver angel dangling between her breasts.

With a laugh, she grabbed the bakery box from the table and took off toward the stairs, leaving Max staring after her with an erection so hard he could barely move.

Mission accomplished.

If he stood right now, he'd be on his knees.

He honestly couldn't remember how long it had been since he'd been crippled by lust. Not since college, at least. But as he pressed his hand to his crotch to stop the blood flow, Max knew he wouldn't settle for anything less ever again.

Josie.

He found her upstairs staring across their alley, looking glorious in the glow of the Tiffany lamp, creamy skin bathed in the light, so lovely. He extended his hand, and she slipped her fingers in his and drew him toward the window.

"Come look at my side of the alley."

He moved to the window, and she stepped into his arms as if she'd waited forever to be there. Her beautiful body aligned smoothly with his, perfectly. "I've wanted to cross this alley from the first night I saw you."

"I wanted you to."

"Could you see me? I wondered."

"Only on the first night when you had the light on. But I could always sense you watching. Sometimes the wind would blow the sheers against your legs, and I'd see you outlined in the darkness. It was very provocative."

She sounded wistful, and he tried to read her expression as she stared through the window. "Are you sorry to see our erotic game end?"

"Yes and no. I wouldn't trade a second of our time together. I've had a wonderful time, Max, but I've always known you'd be leaving."

And that was exactly what Max wanted to hear. She hadn't considered more nights together because she was convinced he wouldn't be here, *not* necessarily because she didn't want more. It was a step in the right direction. "I wouldn't, either."

Josie was about to find out that he wouldn't let her go so easily.

In one move, he scooped her up into his arms.

"Max!" She hung on as he brought her to the bed and deposited her in the middle.

She stretched out in a display of long curves and bare skin. Stepping back, he admired every inch of the vision she made on the holiday comforter, surrounded by red and green pillows.

"I didn't think you could possibly be more lovely than you were from across the alley, but you are," he said.

"You're doing it again."

"What?"

"Saying all the right things." Rolling toward him, she hooked her finger in his belt and pulled him toward her. "Now allow me. I'm tired of being the only naked one around here."

"You're only half-naked, Josette." Capturing her wrist, he stopped her. "It's my turn to strip and your turn to watch."

"Be still my heart. Are you going to perform?"

"You've raised the bar on performances. I couldn't hope to compete."

"No dancing?"

"Just a plain old striptease."

"There is nothing plain or old about you, Max."

The look she swept over him assured him she meant exactly what she said. He liked how she made no bones about how she felt, an emotional honesty from long ago that had always made Josie unique.

"Skin, finally." Hooking her ankles, she watched him with a smile, a vision from his dreams with her breasts popping over the camisole, her bare backside and thigh-high hose.

Her dreamy expression touched him someplace deep, breathed more life into his hope that tonight wouldn't be their only night. Determination spurred him to make his striptease a good one and, inspired, he took his time unbuttoning his shirt, stripping away the sleeves while he turned his back to her.

He tossed his shirt her way. She caught it and rolled it into a pillow that she tucked beneath her cheek. "Your shirt smells like you."

He couldn't touch Josie's dazzling performances, but he made a show of toeing off his shoes and peeling away his pants.

"Oh, Max. The view is fine from back here," she said in a honeyed voice. "I should have insisted you perform and let me watch. I missed out on a bunch."

Max wasn't sure how much he'd have liked standing naked in his grandmother's bedroom with no hope of touching Josie, but he liked the excitement in her voice right now.

Liked that she was close enough to touch.

"Will you do the honors?" He strode toward the bed, smiled when she spun up on her knees so fast that her hair whipped around her shoulders and her breasts swayed enticingly.

"My pleasure."

Slipping her fingers inside his waistband, she maneuvered the briefs over his erection in tantalizing moves. Her hands brushed his skin, made him brace himself against the pleasure that hit hard and fast.

"I should have invited you across the alley sooner," she said.

"We have a lot of anticipation to satisfy in one night."

Whether she agreed or not didn't matter when she trailed her hands down his thighs, dragging the briefs down and exploring the scenery along the way.

Even her simplest touches sent his pulse rate soaring.

She slithered half-off on the bed, until she could reach his feet then motioned him to step out of the briefs. With her sweet backside high in the air, the shimmery hose and stylish pumps enticed him until his erection swelled even harder.

She noticed.

Flinging aside his briefs with a triumphant smile, she slipped her fingers between his thighs, skimmed her way toward his erection.

He grabbed a condom from his wallet and a cookie from the bakery box, then moved back to the bed, set the items down on the nightstand and sank down beside her.

"Looks like you've thought of everything," she said.

"Not quite. I should have brought peppermint flavored condoms."

"I like peppermint."

Her laughter filtered through him, and she reached out to touch him, her fingertips lightly stroking that sensitive place inside his thigh. His erection jumped toward her hand like a heat-seeking missile, and she twirled a fingertip along his length, a smile on her lips as she dipped down to flick her tongue over the head in a wet stroke.

Her touch galvanized him, and it took him a full minute to realize that if he let her take control of him now, he'd never get it back. So he caught her against him, and she went over in a fluid roll, let him maneuver her against him into a position that fitted them neatly against each other. Side by side. His face to that sweet place between her thighs. Her face to his.

"Can you guess what cookie this is?" he asked, dragging his tongue a lazy stroke over the trimmed hairs at the apex of her thighs, savoring the almost taste of her heat.

Exhaling a shuddering breath, she shivered when he dragged his tongue over her again.

Then stretched out and grabbed the cookie, then dropped it onto her stomach, where it landed icing side up.

69.

He met her gaze over the expanse of her beautiful body. "I've waited a long time to touch you."

"Me, too, Max. Me, too."

EACH TOUCH of his mouth on her skin, each touch of his strong hands caressing her body felt unreal. Even in her wildest fantasies, Josie couldn't have imagined the reality of Max in her bed, the way his eyes glinted with purpose as he lowered his face between her thighs....

The first brush of his mouth made her jump, a wild reaction of anticipation, and surprise. He shouldered his way between her thighs boldly, nestled himself into a comfortable position as though he planned to stay a good long while.

His smile vanished as he went down again for another tantalizing taste, only this time he dragged his tongue along her moist folds, a delicious stroke that made her quiver. He seemed attuned to her every reaction, knew when to tease and when to let her catch her breath.

And when he wiggled his tongue inside, pushed deep

with a lazy stroke, he had her digging her fingers into the comforter to hang on. He pleasured her with a skill that made her nearly forget that she had a part to play here, too. But how could she do anything but hold on tight as he licked, nibbled and sucked his way along her sex with that lethal mouth?

She stretched out against him and distracted herself with his gorgeous body. Dragging her hands along his legs, through the smattering of silky hairs along his hard thighs, she grazed the backs of his knees with erotic touches. He shivered, and she smiled. He was ticklish.

She hadn't read that in the business section.

Although she'd known this man her whole life, there were so many things about him that were total mysteries. She'd never felt that lack more than right now, with her fingers exploring his, with her cheek resting against his thigh, with her mouth brushing kisses along his skin.

He had gorgeous legs, long and not overly muscled, but she couldn't remember ever noticing them before, and she'd spent her fair share of time looking at him. But now she admired him with a woman's sight, experienced him with a woman's responses.

But nothing in her experience had prepared her for his mouth working magic between her thighs, and she moaned when he caught that little bud between his lips. Josie grabbed his calves and hung on as he indulged that place where every nerve ending seemed wired. Ribbons of fire curled in on themselves and made her burn.

It wasn't until his erection bumped her cheek that she remembered the missed opportunity here, and in a lightning-fast move, she zeroed in on her target.

Wrapping her fingers around him, she guided him toward her mouth…. In one slow pull, she took control. She explored the hot velvet hardness of an erection that was as sculpted and beautiful as the rest of him.

He let out a low groan, and his whole body gathered tight in reply. She delighted making him react to her touch. Then he redoubled his efforts until she squirmed, too, with need.

She made love to his erection, sucking him inside as far as she could. Tonight was all about making memories, and she wanted Max *always* to remember their night together.

She used her hands to assist each stroke, creating a suck zone on the upstroke before releasing him in a dance of wet tongue and nibbling teeth. She fondled his velvety scrotum in her palm, explored his intimate places with curious fingers.

She thrilled when he rocked his hips, a gentle thrusting that proved she was driving him wild, wearing away his careful control and pushing him closer to the edge.

But Josie should have known that Max would give as good as he got. He sank a finger deep inside her, and they started a rhythm that mimed lovemaking, her knees clinging to his head, his hips indolently thrusting.

Hunger mounted, liquid heat that surged through her, fantasies transforming into stunning reality, more incredible than imagination could have ever allowed. A mind-numbing pleasure, the sort that dissolved her into a mass of greedy impulses, her sex clenching in needy bursts that made her ride his mouth.

And Max knew, oh, he knew exactly what to do. Thrusting his tongue deep, he slithered his finger backward, pushing her impossibly farther, applying just the right pressure, touching, thrusting….

Then Josie came apart again, spasms that burst as weltering heat inside, made her lose the rhythm as she rode the ache, the pleasure crashing in on her over and over simply because Max wouldn't stop.

6

JOSIE DIDN'T REMEMEBER when she lost hold of his erection, but when her heartbeat finally slowed its gallop and she could open her eyes again, she found her cheek resting comfortably against that pulsing hard length.

"I thought it was my turn," she managed to get out.

Max peered up from between her thighs with a satisfied smile. "I told you, fair's only fair. You've had me on my knees for weeks. I've got some catching up to do."

Josie wasn't on her knees but on her back, where she would likely stay until this dreamy languor wore off. But that would require too much energy to explain, so she just exhaled heavily and closed her eyes again.

Max disentangled himself and maneuvered around until he could pull on a condom. Then he reached for her.

It took a few boneless maneuvers, but she finally lay draped on top of him, her hair cloaking them like a blanket. As much as she liked being cocooned together, she could only rally enough energy to kiss his throat.

"You killed me," she said, deciding there was no point in denying the obvious.

She just held her mouth poised above the pulse point that beat so steadily beneath his skin and savored the feel of his arms around her, his body spread sexily underneath her, all male hardness and strength.

"You feel alive to me, Josette." And to prove his point, he raked his hands down her back, cupped her bottom with both hands and ground against her with a needy erection.

Miraculously, her sex gave a moist throb in reply.

"Life signs. Who knew?"

"Told you." He breathed the words against her ear and won another achy response from a body that couldn't decide whether to ride that hard length or roll over and play dead.

She didn't have much time to decide. The clock ticked on, and while she'd always known Max would be leaving for his high-powered life again, somehow right now, while lying satisfied in his arms, she regretted all the potential opportunities to climax over and over again she would miss.

So many possibilities… Snuggling close on New Year's Eve while the sky filled with fireworks… On Valentine's Day wearing the sexy red lingerie he'd sent her… In the middle of the night while they were drowsy… At dawn when they awakened in each other's arms to greet the new day.

Max didn't give her time to dwell on this change of mood. Flashing a smile of pure promise, he worked his way inside her wet heat in one long, slow, push that stretched and filled her until she could only gasp.

Josie thought he'd annihilated her with that last orgasm, but she was wrong. All it took was his body stretched underneath hers, his hot length inside, and he not only proved she was alive, but on fire.

Then he began to move.

Drawing out almost completely, he pushed back in another stunning stroke. She moaned this time, and he caught the sound on a kiss. Thrusting his tongue deep, he mirrored the motion of his hips until thoughts fell away, and she knew nothing but the feel of the man underneath her, *inside* her.

He started up a sultry rhythm with long, lingering strokes that brought her back to life. Wrapping her arms tightly around him, she braced her knees tight to hang on, and met his kiss with a demand of her own.

Those other orgasms had been foreplay compared to what was building now. And Josie rode this glorious wave, her body surging as she raked her hands over him, crushed her breasts to his chest with each driving stroke. She finally sank her fingers into his shoulders to hang on, amazed by her response to him, by the urgency that dragged her from her daze.

She met him stroke for luscious stroke, awed by how their bodies came together as if they'd waited forever for the privilege. And perhaps they had. She'd lusted after Max for so long…and she'd teased him mercilessly across the alley. Was it any wonder why they came together now as if they'd been made for each other, as if this pulsing rhythm she experienced could only happen in his arms?

Her answer lay in each sweet stroke that made her body want, made her mouth seek his wildly, made her ride that ache even harder.

Max must have known, too. He bombarded her with sensation, grazing his hands along her ribs, zeroing in on her breasts. Cupping her in his palms, he caught her nipples and tugged hard. More pleasure crashed through her, and she moaned, the sound escaping in a raspy burst that won a growl from him.

His restraint wavered when he trailed his mouth down her throat, a barrage of kissing and nibbling and tasting that left fire in his wake. Arching against him, she braced her thighs tight, used her weight to roll to her side.

Max caught her around the waist before he slid out. He

thrust back inside hard enough to force the breath from her lungs, and she gasped as he dragged them over in one strong, contained move.

Suddenly, he was on top, his broad shoulders blocking out the world. She could only stare up into his beautiful face, memorize each detail, the hunger that sharpened his features, the pleasure that made his gaze caress her as if she'd honored him with the privilege.

A memory to last a lifetime.

That thought spurred her to action. Arching her hips upward to take him deeper, she dug her fingers into his bottom to ride each stroke longer, harder, testing his control.

And she knew she'd pushed too far when he ground out a throaty growl and sank his fingers into her bottom to speed up their pace. He buried his face in her hair, his cheek against hers, and for long stunning moments they could only hang on to each other as they came together in a pleasure so intense they couldn't stop thrusting, couldn't stop riding a crest that was unlike anything she'd ever experienced before.

Then she lay wrapped tight in his arms, trying to catch her breath while their Christmas Eve moon rose higher above their alley, and Josie wished this night would never end.

She'd expected to satisfy her desire for this man during this night together, but as she lay in his arms, she knew she wanted him to be so much more than her Christmas fantasy.

She wanted this man for a lifetime.

MAX TRIED TO fake bravado, tried to act as if his climax, an explosion of every nerve in his body, wasn't monumental. Josie thought he was a one-night stand, but he'd been leveled by this woman in so many ways. His heart had never pounded so hard, his legs had never vibrated so furiously.

So he just held her close, buried his face in her hair and told himself to get a grip. He'd never get a shot at another five minutes if he scared Josie off by coming on too strong.

"Let's go downstairs and open gifts," she finally said through a yawn.

Unable to resist, he ran his fingers along her cheek, traced the corner of lips reddened by his kisses. "Not tired?"

"I'll make coffee. I refuse to waste a second of our night together *sleeping*." With that, she scooted out of his arms and tugged at the blanket underneath him. "Come on. You don't want to sleep, do you?"

"No, Josie. I don't want to sleep." Not until he was assured he wouldn't get the boot in the morning. Grabbing the blanket, he rolled off the bed. "I'm all yours."

For as long as she'd have him.

He'd no sooner wrapped the blanket around her than she took off toward the door, leaving him standing on legs still obscenely weak from lovemaking.

"Grab the pillows. I'll get more blankets," she shot back over her shoulder before disappearing into the hall.

He couldn't decide how to interpret her eagerness. On one level he was flattered. By her own admission, she didn't want to waste a second, but there was something else. Josie was almost *too* determined, and he wanted to interpret that to mean she didn't want to think about tomorrow.

Because she knew he'd disappoint her?

She had every right to think he would. He'd done nothing in the past ten years to make her, or anyone from his past for that matter, think he could have a change of heart.

He hadn't let anyone know he still had a heart.

Max had no easy answers, but he could hope. And use every means he could think of to get her to talk to him.

Unfortunately, Josie didn't want to talk.

By the time he joined her in the living room, she'd fashioned them a comfortable nest beneath the Christmas tree. He dropped the pillows in the middle then talked her out of coffee in favor of hot cocoa like his grandmother used to make them long ago.

He only had a few tricks up his sleeve right now, and their shared past topped the list. Sex was a close second.

He'd use both to get what he wanted.

Josie.

When he returned from the kitchen with two steaming mugs, she accepted hers with a smile. "You remembered I like extra marshmallows."

"Hard to forget when you used to hog the entire bag."

"Hog?" she demanded, but he could see the smile twitching around her mouth that he'd pleased her by remembering, which was another step in the right direction as far as he was concerned. "I never hogged the marshmallows."

"You made me look generous with my 'love note' sugar cookies."

"I don't think so."

"A matter of opinion."

"A matter of memory, and a faulty one at that."

He set his mug on the nearby coffee table and sank to the floor beside her, enjoying the way she looked breathless and lovely with the blanket tucked under her arms, her shoulders bare in the twinkling lights.

She'd replaced the music with another CD of Christmas carols, and he watched her rummage under the tree while a version of "O Holy Night" played softly in the background. The gift was small and neatly wrapped with foil paper and a bright bow, and he felt that long-forgotten zip of pleasure again when she handed him the present.

"Merry Christmas, Max."

She'd already gifted him with so much more than she could possibly know, but now wasn't the time to share that. So he just accepted the gift and removed the wrapping.

Scooting onto her knees, she watched him, scarcely containing her excitement, and he stared down into the box to find a gold ornament in the shape of a star.

The photograph in the middle showed Josie, Lucas and their parents along with Max and his grandmother in front of a twenty-foot tall Christmas tree that he recognized as Court du Chaud's own. That tree still stood in the courtyard and had for as far back as Max could remember. It was court tradition.

Each weekend after Thanksgiving, the residents would erect and decorate the tree. The men climbed up on the ladders to string lights. The women provided a feast of holiday goodies and supervised what always turned into a weekend-long party. They'd repeat the whole process again after the New Year to take the tree down.

He recognized the year, too—the Christmas before he and Lucas had gone off to college. They'd been applying to colleges and caught up in the full swing of being seniors raring to graduate, planning for the future. They'd all been one big happy family then—it hadn't been until a few years later that he and Lucas had run into trouble and all their lives had changed.

He stared down at his grandmother's image. She'd been old for as long as he could remember, but while packing up the house, he'd come across photos of her in her youth. He'd barely recognized the beautiful woman she'd once been, a very striking stranger who'd lived and loved and given so many years to him.

Josie's parents looked the same as they always had, while he and Lucas looked carefree and full of themselves. Max couldn't help feeling regret for the closeness they'd lost. But he'd talked to Lucas and started the ball rolling on working his way back toward the people he'd cared about. Another start.

Then there was Josie... He stared into her young face, so familiar even with the wild hair and glinting braces.

Despite the events of the past few weeks, he was more familiar with this young face than the gorgeous woman who stared expectantly at him through the same green eyes. This woman had captivated him when he'd least expected to be captivated, when he hadn't realized how much he needed to let himself feel again.

"A Christmas keepsake from a happy time." He understood what she wanted to do here. The gesture was typical Josie, and her caring hadn't changed as she'd grown. "You don't want me to leave again and forget."

She gave a casual shrug, and he knew she had no idea that he would never be able to forget what he'd found with her, whether she gifted him with a keepsake or not.

He wanted past, present and future.

"I just want you to know that you always have people who love you, Max. Even Lucas. He's another one who's drowning himself with work." She gave a wry laugh. "I don't know what happened between you all those years ago, and it's not important anymore. I just know that whenever your name comes up, whenever we come across a picture of you together, Lucas is sad. He doesn't have to say anything. I see it, and it breaks my heart."

He saw his opportunity to come clean about the past, but Josie cut him off when she pressed a kiss to his mouth and whispered against his lips. "Maybe if you have an ornament to remind you, you'll send me a Christmas card so I won't have to read the newspaper to find out how you're doing. I don't have Nana anymore to fill in the blanks."

Her words shamed him in ways he hadn't known he could be shamed. She thought he could make love to her and then walk away. What hurt most was that until his return to Court du Chaud, until she'd seduced him across the alley, she'd have been right. He'd traveled so far from everything she considered important. He *had* forgotten.

But Josie was helping him remember.

"Now it's your turn." Hanging the ornament on the tree, he pulled out one of the gifts he'd brought for her.

She made short work of the gift-wrapped box, and he found her enthusiasm charming as she lifted out the stack of yellowed love letters bound in gold ribbon. "What are these, Max?"

"*Real* love notes. I was reading them the first night I saw you across the alley."

"Nana's?"

He nodded.

"She told me so much about falling in love with your grandfather. They sounded like quite a pair. I was always sorry that I never knew them together."

"Me, too."

Her smile grew wistful. "Are you sure you want me to have these?"

"Yes, and my grandmother would want you to have them, too. She loved you. Even though I didn't visit often enough, I was in constant contact with her. I can't tell you how many times I wanted to bring someone in to help her, a companion with some medical training, someone who'd keep an eye on her and do all the things she couldn't. I didn't like her living alone."

"I'm sure Nana would have no part of that."

"You're not kidding. She told me if I sent anyone, she simply wouldn't let them in. She had you right next door, and that was all she wanted." Slipping his hand over hers, he threaded their fingers together. "Thank you for caring so much and for being here for her when I wasn't."

Josie lifted her gaze to his, and those beautiful green eyes glistened with tears. "She always knew how much you loved her, Max. Don't ever question that."

Lifting her hand, he brushed his mouth across her knuckles, grateful for the reassurance he didn't deserve. "I wish she knew that I've been rethinking so many of my choices."

"Have you?"

"I've realized a lot since coming home, about where my life has been heading and where I'd like it to go."

"I'm sure she knows. And she'd be happy." A tear rolled down her cheek, and he thumbed it away, couldn't resist pulling her into his arms.

She melted against him, and he held her close, feeling connected by grief for the woman who'd been such an important part of their lives.

When Josie lifted her mouth to his, the taste of tears in her kiss, Max unwrapped the blanket she wore, exposing her creamy skin beneath the jeweled Christmas lights. He touched her almost reverently, reassured her in the only way he could—through the magic they made in each other's arms.

7

THE BLARE OF THE telephone jarred Josie from sleep, and she opened her eyes and looked around, drowsy and disoriented. She lay tangled around Max on the floor in the living room, his knee buried snugly between hers, his arm possessively around her waist. The light seeping through the plantation shutters revealed their night together had finally ended.

They must have fallen asleep after making love, but Josie didn't get a chance to feel disappointed for the wasted dawn when the phone rang again. Max stirred sleepily beside her, tried to pull her closer, but she slipped away, scooting across the floor to lift the receiver.

Grabbing a throw from the couch, she wrapped it around her and glanced at the display. "Merry Christmas, Lucas."

"Merry Christmas, sunshine. You should be here with us. As usual Mom made enough cranberry pancakes to feed the block, and she's expecting me to eat yours and mine."

Josie laughed. Cranberry pancakes were a tradition with the Russells, just as celebrating Christmas together. They rotated between her home in New Orleans, her parents' in Florida and Lucas's on the West Coast. She'd intended to head to her parents this year, too, but had made up a last-minute excuse to spend the holiday with Max.

"I wish I was there, but I just couldn't get away." Okay, a little white lie. When she eyed the man stretching contentedly on the floor, the blanket falling aside to reveal his toned thighs and tight belly and the yummy terrain in between, she hadn't *wanted* to get away. "You know how it is sometimes."

There was a beat of silence on the other end and then, "Oh, I do. I *really* do."

There was something in his voice…something that sounded suspiciously smug. But Josie didn't get a chance to dwell on what her brother might be lording over her because Max chose that moment to roll toward her in a breathtaking display of shifting muscle, tanned skin and dangling parts.

Pressing her finger to his lips, she gestured him to stay quiet. About the last thing she needed right now was Lucas hearing a man's voice, and not just any man, but *this* man.

"Did my gifts arrive?" She tried to sound casual as he twirled his tongue around her finger before sucking it inside his mouth suggestively.

He shot her a purely roguish grin, and her whole body melted on a wave of awareness that made her glad she was sitting. Amazing how he could affect her when she still felt achy and satisfied from all their sex last night.

"I'm sorry, Lucas. What did you just say?"

"I said your gifts arrived. Is everything all right? You sound distracted."

"No, no, everything's fine. So did you like the computer game?"

"Can't wait to play it, but I want to know where you found a computer game about Captain Gabriel Dampier and his pirates. From a local company? I didn't recognize the name."

And Lucas would know. As the owner of his own software empire that wrote programs for law enforcement agencies all over the country, he had a bead on the industry. "Actually, Thibault Enterprises is a one-man operation. John Thibault is a computer geek I know from school. I had him write the program."

Lucas laughed. "Only you, sunshine. I suppose you wanted to remind me that I owe you a Mardi Gras visit this year."

"Of course. I'm Krewe du Chaud's president, and I've got everyone I know on the float committee. We're building the captain's ship. Wait until you see it. It's absolutely brilliant."

"Wouldn't miss it. Now Mom's chomping at the bit to talk to you, so before I pass you off, let me talk to Max."

Josie blinked. "Wh-what?"

"Max," Lucas repeated. "There's something I need to tell him before Mom gets you on the line. I'll never get a chance then. He is there, isn't he?"

"How did you know?"

There was a beat of silence on the other end. "He didn't tell you?"

"Tell me what? You've talked to him?" She stared at Max, who gazed back unrepentant.

Josie couldn't decide whether to hand him the phone or hit him with it. Surely he wouldn't have told Lucas about their fantasy night?

"Put him on the line. I want to give him a Christmas present. You can call Mom and Dad back later."

She covered the receiver. "Did Lucas tell you where I keep my spare key?"

Max nodded and, scowling, she handed him the phone,

smelling a big fat setup that reminded her of days long gone by. Or so she'd thought.

Curling up against the sofa, she tried to make sense of the one-sided conversation.

"I plan to tell her," he said. "But I wanted to give her a Christmas gift first. You called before we got around to it."

Josie watched as Max cocked his head to the side, listening to Lucas on the other end before he said, "Okay. Tell me."

Whatever Lucas said sent a play of emotions across Max's face, and she was forced to sit there watching, burning with curiosity while Max held the phone in a white-knuckled grip.

"No, I had no clue," he finally said. "I'm sorry you thought I did. But, well, at least everything makes sense now."

What was *everything?* Josie wanted to ask, especially when he lifted his gaze to hers. The transformation was amazing. In a heartbeat the tension on his face melted into a smile.

A very satisfied smile.

"Apology accepted. How long did you say again?" he spoke into the receiver. "That long?" He gave a laugh. "Call it the oblivion of youth, but I was way too self-absorbed to notice. And, yes, sometimes things do change."

Josie turned away and blinked hard against the tears threatening to fall. Listening to him talking with Lucas again was like an unexpected Christmas gift. While she didn't know what Max had told Lucas about them, she considered anything that brought these two together a good thing.

Max finally ended the call, and she felt his hand on her shoulder, felt him squeeze gently.

"You okay?" he asked.

She turned toward him, suddenly back in control. How could she not be with Max and Lucas up to their old tricks again, ganging up on her? Josie wasn't anyone's pesky kid sister anymore, and Max would do well to recognize it.

"I'm fine," she said. "But I want some answers. What's going on? What do you want to tell me, and when did you talk to Lucas? You didn't say anything about what's going on between us, did you?"

Max knelt before her, took her hands in his. "Deep breath, and I'll explain."

"Just tell me."

"I called Lucas right after you accepted my invitation for Christmas Eve and, no, I didn't tell him anything about us except that we wanted to resume our friendship."

"I thought we agreed to keep the past and the family out of *us*."

"You came up with that rule when I got here last night. I didn't agree to anything. I couldn't because I'd already talked to Lucas."

"You didn't mention that."

He smiled. "Would have ruined the surprise."

"What surprise?" She scowled harder. "Please explain what's happening here because I don't understand what you're doing."

He squeezed her hands a little tighter. "I'm not interested in one night with you, Josie. We've found something special and, if you're interested, I'd like to see where it leads."

"But..." Her voice trailed off as full impact of that statement hit. "See where *what* leads? You live in New York and I live here."

"I own the company. I make home base wherever I

want. And being home again has made me look at all the reasons I've stayed away. They don't seem like very good reasons anymore."

"Are these some of the decisions you mentioned last night? Are you thinking of relocating?"

He nodded.

She could only stare at him, not at all sure what to make of this turn of events. She hadn't considered more than a night together, hadn't dared to go there.

"What did Lucas want you to tell me?" she asked, stalling, needing time to sort through this crazy feeling suddenly ballooning inside, making it hard to draw a decent breath.

"The reason we fought."

"Now? After all these years?"

"You need to know. I did something that I thought was a good thing, but Lucas didn't agree. Now I understand why."

Lifting the chain around her neck, he fingered the silver angel with a strange smile.

There was something so wistful about his expression, something so wry and amused…then it hit her. "You were my secret Santa."

He nodded, meeting her gaze with a wealth of emotion, and she vividly remembered that Christmas. A hallmark year for memories she'd rather forget.

Except for her secret Santa.

School had hosted an annual Yule ball. It was a festive and much anticipated event, and since Josie had made Christmas her signature holiday, she'd headed up the decorating committee. She'd cooked up a beautiful Victorian Christmas theme, which the board had embraced. For months, she and her team had worked their hearts out plotting and planning the event, had even convinced the city to lend them some Mardi Gras decorations to recreate New Orleans at the turn of the century.

She'd been sixteen and wildly excited about the ball. She'd also been the only one in her circle of acquaintances who hadn't had a date.

Remembering back to that thoroughly forgettable time, Josie honestly couldn't blame any of her fellow classmates for not asking her out. She'd been what Nana had called a "late bloomer" and still cringed at pictures from that painful year.

Orthodontia, contact lenses and a capable dermatologist had eventually cleared up the most obvious problems, but the memory of that sad and lonely holiday…

"Why would you be my secret Santa, Max? You sent me a gift every day for the twelve days before Christmas. And they were such thoughtful gifts."

He stared down at the silver angel. "I saw you in the Quarter on the night of the Yule ball. You were standing on a street corner all dressed up, chatting and smoking cigarettes with a bunch of vagrants."

Another of her more stellar moments. She'd vowed to go to her ball stag but had copped out when she'd seen the grand hall in the old Jackson building transformed into a glittering world from a bygone era. She'd been the head of the decorating committee, *noticeable,* and had felt so ugly and pathetic in a room filled with couples dancing the night away.

She'd headed into the Quarter, instead, bought a few packs of cigarettes and made friends with some homeless folks who roamed the streets between Rue de Royale and Rue de Chartres.

"You were there when I came home, Max. You knew I lied to my parents about what a great time I had?"

He nodded.

"But what was Lucas's problem with you being my secret Santa? That's the *only* decent thing that happened to me that Christmas. He should have appreciated how nice you were."

Max rested the angel against her neck, sat back and met her gaze squarely. "I never told Lucas because I didn't want him to think I was being stupid. He always thought I was a wimp when it came to you."

"You were *nice*. There's a difference."

He inclined his head. "Apparently Lucas didn't think so. When he found out, he went nuts. He was angrier than I'd ever seen him."

"Angry about what?"

"He told me I'd crossed the line. He made it sound like I was taking advantage of you with some dirty ulterior motive for sending those gifts. I couldn't believe he'd even think that, when I only wanted to make you feel better."

Max shrugged, a casual gesture that Josie saw right through. Ten years later, and he still hurt.

"Max—"

"I mean, come on, Josie, you were sixteen and I was nearly out of college. My head definitely wasn't *there,* but Lucas wouldn't believe me. I felt like I'd done something horrible and failed everyone—my grandmother, your parents, everyone who believed in me—and I felt like I needed to prove myself.

"It took me a while, but I've finally figured out that I only needed to prove myself to me. It wasn't about the fight with Lucas or playing your secret Santa. I felt as if I didn't deserve everything your family had given me through the years, everything my grandmother sacrificed to raise me. But at the time…"

"Oh, Max—" But she suddenly didn't have any words.

Reaching under the tree, he grabbed the last gift and handed it to her. "It's all in here. Open it."

Her heart aching, Josie peeled away the bow and wrapping to find another box of letters. These weren't yellowed or brittle with age. The envelopes were new, the whole stack wrapped in festive red and green ribbon, with dates written in Max's bold hand.

She opened the one on the top, dated the night she'd first danced for him. *Ma chérie,* the letter began…

"It's in French."

"French is a romance language." He smiled. "I told you I was thinking about more than *notre nuit pour la fantaisie.*"

The words tumbled from his lips as easily as they always had, but she skimmed the page, struggling to understand his fluent French. She recognized just enough to know his letter explained his reaction to her performance after she'd turned out the lights. He wrote of his surprise, his arousal and the way wanting her had made him think about the past.

"I wanted you to understand everything I figured out while I've been home, all you'd come to mean to me. I want a chance to explore what we have together, Josie. I don't want you to say *'au revoir'* after that incredible night we just spent together."

That crazy feeling kept on swelling until she could barely breathe.

And Max knew. "So what do you say? Interested in seeing what we can have together?"

Josie loved surprises, and this unexpected Christmas surprise was better than anything she'd ever received. Slipping her arms around him, she held him close. "Yes."

A simple word because there wasn't anything else to say.

She'd never considered more than a night with Max because she hadn't believed one would be possible, and she refused to set herself up to be disappointed. But having the chance to know him again, a chance to explore all this wild arousal and these oh-so right feelings... Lifting her face to his, she kissed him to seal the deal.

His mouth covered hers, a kiss that echoed everything she'd discovered in his arms last night, a kiss that made her want.

But a thought occurred to her, and she broke away.

"You still haven't told me why Lucas thought you were taking advantage of me. He's not stupid, so I'm not buying that he thought you were interested in me with any *dirty ulterior motive*."

"I wish I'd have been so smart."

"Really, Max. Think about it. I looked heinous at sixteen. The braces and my horrible skin—"

"You were still you, Josie."

More simple words, more *right* words that revealed so much about this man, about how much he cared and always had. He might have left Court du Chaud and lost his way during the years, but he was still Max.

"That was what Lucas called to tell me," Max explained. "Apparently, he wasn't worried about *me*. From what he just told me on the phone, he was worried about *your* reaction if you found out I'd been sending the gifts."

Oh, no!

Josie knew what was coming and squeezed her eyes tightly shut. She covered her ears for good measure. No good. Max was stronger, and craftier. Grabbing both her hands, he brought them to his lips.

"What I didn't know when I'd decided to play your secret Santa was that you had a huge crush on me. Lucas thought I knew how you felt. He was afraid that if you found out I was sending the gifts you'd think I was interested and get hurt."

She opened her eyes and gazed into his smiling eyes. "You weren't supposed to ever know that."

"Well, I didn't have a clue until he just told me on the phone. His apology was my Christmas gift." He laughed softly, his breath bursting softly against her skin. "Your brother is as sick as ever."

"Oh, Max. I know it seems silly now. I mean, it's been so long, and we've shared so much these past few weeks. But I'm glad you didn't know that I moon-pied after you."

He pulled her into his arms, so she could feel all his hard places, thrill at the promise of the days ahead. "I like that you wanted me then. I like that you want me now."

"I do, and I can't wait to read all my love letters. Yours and Nana's. But I'll need help translating yours, you know."

"Looking forward to it." He ran a finger along her bare shoulder, pressed a kiss to the top of her head. "We're going to have fun, Josette. I promise."

She believed him, and when she spotted the white bakery box on the end table, she leaned up to rummage through the cookies until she found the one she wanted.

Unwrap me.

Thank you, Chloe!

Handing him the cookie, she said, "Christmas is getting on here, Max. I think it's time you opened another gift."

"Me, too. And it'll be the best gift of them all."

Josie sighed. He always said exactly the right thing, and did the right thing. Reaching for her, he unwrapped the blanket with a flourish that rivaled any of her performances.

"Merry Christmas, Max."

"Merry Christmas, Josie."

Then his hands came around her, and when he caught her lips in a possessive kiss, Josie knew she'd been right.... Magic was happening around Court du Chaud this Christmas.

* * * * *

Look for Jeanie London's next
RED LETTER NIGHTS *story,*
Going All Out
*coming in January 2007
from Mills & Boon Blaze®.*

MILLS & BOON
Live the emotion

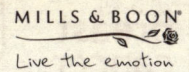

Blaze

GIVE ME FEVER by Karen Anders
Red Letter Nights

When Tally Addison's brother goes missing, she knows who to turn to – gorgeous ex-cop Christien Castille. Only, when she and Christien stumble into a search for hidden treasure, she discovers she's already found hers…in him!

THE COWBOY WAY by Candace Schuler

Jo Beth Bensen is practical. Burned once by a cowboy, she swore never to get involved with another one. But sexy Clay Madison is different, and just too easy on the eyes to ignore. Her body needs some sexual relief, and the cowboy way is the only way to go…

INDECENT SUGGESTION by Elizabeth Bevarly

It's supposed to help them stop smoking. But the hypnosis session Turner McCloud and Becca Mercer attend hasn't worked. However, since then, the just-friends couple can't keep their hands off each other!

ALL I WANT… by Isabel Sharpe
The Wrong Bed

Krista Marlow wanted two things for Christmas – a sexy man and a lasting relationship. Well, she got the sexy man one night when she and Seth Wellington ended up in bed in the same cosy cabin. But would the relationship survive once Seth revealed his true identity?

On sale 3rd November 2006

Available at WHSmith, Tesco, ASDA, Borders, Eason, Sainsbury's and most bookshops

www.millsandboon.co.uk

BCC/AD 2006 a

breast cancer CAMPAIGN

researching the cure

The facts you need to know:

- Breast cancer is the commonest form of cancer in the United Kingdom. **One woman in nine** will develop the disease during her lifetime.

- Each year around **41,000** women and approximately **300** men are diagnosed with breast cancer and around **13,000** women and **90** men will die from the disease.

- 80% of all breast cancers occur in post-menopausal women and approximately 8,200 pre-menopausal women are diagnosed with the disease each year.

- However, survival rates are improving, with on average 77.5% of women diagnosed between 1996 and 1999 still alive five years later, compared to 72.8% for women diagnosed between 1991 and 1996.

Breast Cancer Campaign is the only charity that specialises in funding independent breast cancer research throughout the UK. It aims to find the cure for breast cancer by funding research which looks at improving diagnosis and treatment of breast cancer, better understanding how it develops and ultimately either curing the disease or preventing it.

MILLS & BOON®

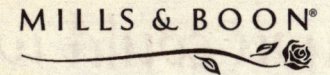

BCC/AD 2006 b

During the month of October Harlequin Mills & Boon will donate 10p from the sale of every Modern Romance™ series book to help Breast Cancer Campaign continue *researching the cure*.

Statistics cannot describe the impact of the disease on the lives of those who are affected by it and on their families and friends.

Do your part to help, visit <u>www.breastcancercampaign.org</u> and make a donation today.

breast cancer CAMPAIGN

researching the cure

Breast Cancer Campaign is a charity registered by the Charity Commission for England and Wales (Charity No. 299758), whose registered office is Clifton Centre, 110 Clifton Street, London, EC2A 4HT.
Tel: 020 7749 3700 Fax: 020 7749 3701

1106/XMAS TITLES a

All you could want for Christmas!

Meet handsome and seductive men under the mistletoe, escape to the world of Regency romance or simply relax by the fire with a heartwarming tale by one of our bestselling authors. These special stories will fill your holiday with Christmas sparkle!

On sale 6th October 2006

On sale 20th October 2006

1106/XMAS TITLES b

On sale
3rd November
2006

On sale 17th November 2006

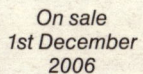

On sale
1st December
2006

Available at
WHSmith, Asda,
Tesco and all good bookshops

www.millsandboon.co.uk

M&B

2 FREE

BOOKS AND A SURPRISE GIFT!

We would like to take this opportunity to thank you for reading this Mills & Boon® book by offering you the chance to take TWO more specially selected titles from the Blaze™ series absolutely FREE! We're also making this offer to introduce you to the benefits of the Mills & Boon® Reader Service™—

- ★ FREE home delivery
- ★ FREE gifts and competitions
- ★ FREE monthly Newsletter
- ★ Exclusive Reader Service offers
- ★ Books available before they're in the shops

Accepting these FREE books and gift places you under no obligation to buy, you may cancel at any time, even after receiving your free shipment. Simply complete your details below and return the entire page to the address below. You don't even need a stamp!

YES! Please send me 2 free Blaze books and a surprise gift. I understand that unless you hear from me, I will receive 4 superb new titles every month for just £3.10 each, postage and packing free. I am under no obligation to purchase any books and may cancel my subscription at any time. The free books and gift will be mine to keep in any case.

K6ZED

Ms/Mrs/Miss/Mr .... Initials ....

BLOCK CAPITALS PLEASE

Surname ....

Address ....

....

.... Postcode ....

Send this whole page to:
UK: FREEPOST CN81, Croydon, CR9 3WZ

Offer valid in UK only and is not available to current Mills & Boon® Reader Service™ subscribers to this series. Overseas and Eire please write for details. We reserve the right to refuse an application and applicants must be aged 18 years or over. Only one application per household. Terms and prices subject to change without notice. Offer expires 31st January 2007. As a result of this application, you may receive offers from Harlequin Mills & Boon and other carefully selected companies. If you would prefer not to share in this opportunity please write to The Data Manager, PO Box 676, Richmond, TW9 1WU.

Mills & Boon® is a registered trademark owned by Harlequin Mills & Boon Limited.
Blaze ™ is being used as a trademark. The Mills & Boon® Reader Service™ is being used as a trademark.